A SUMMER WITH Charlie

A SUMMER WITH Charlie

Richard Edward Noble

Revised Edition

ISBN 978-0-9798085-6-2

Published in the United States of America

By

Noble Publishing,
889 C.C. Land Road, Eastpoint, Fl. 32328

Interior layout and design by
Carol Noble

Cover layout and design by Graphic designer
Diane Beauvais Dyal

DEDICATION

This book is dedicated to Richard Anderson Sr.

Dick is an old friend. He was born and raised in good old Lawrence, Massachusetts, my hometown and the setting for this story. The scenes, the places, the conversations, the characters and even the ideas expressed are as much a part of him as they are of me.

I've known Dick since I was a small child. We've always stayed in touch through the years. He has been a friend, a confidant and my neighbor at times. We have had many an interesting discussion on the "big stuff" and the "small stuff."

Thank-you my friend, your friendship and support have always been an inspiration.

INTRODUCTION

This is one of those stories that is supposed to make you cry. If you read it and you don't cry you're a better man than I am, Charlie Brown! This is a short story, but it tags all the bases. It deals with the "big stuff." It deals with life, love, morality, sex, death, religion, friendship, boys and girls, growing up, home, neighborhood and country. For me it is a trip down memory lane. It's the old days, the old places and the old gang. Despite the seriousness of the subject matter, it is a story of memories, youth and laughter.

I feel like a scientist observing the universe in this book. I can tell you about the planets and the stars. I can theorize and analyze. I can tell you a lot of things. I can explain to you a lot of stuff. I can describe events in detail. I can tell you how. I can tell you where. I can tell you when. But I can't tell you why.

When I was young, I thought of love as a passion. It was a drive, a compulsion, even, in some strange ways, a duty. Now that I am old, I don't know what it is. I don't know why it is. I observe it once again like the scientist observing the planets. I don't know why it happens. I don't know where it comes from. I have no explanation for that look in a girl or boy's eye; for all those mysterious feelings.

I once thought that it was all about hormones. All my hormones have pretty much dried up and have now turned into liver spots; yet I still love. I still have love. I realize now that life is, as the philosophers say, a phenomenon. Death is the same.

I recently read a book by a man who had lived through both World Wars. He saw a lot of men and women executed. He wrote a section on observing how they reacted to the experience. How some went off kicking and screaming; how some were defiant; how some fell to their knees and begged. Instead of naming this book, *A Summer with Charlie*, it could just as well have been called, *Watching Charlie Die*.

In my life, I have watched a lot of friends, relatives and loved ones die. I have witnessed them turn like the leaves of autumn. I have seen them change from living, laughing, vibrant things, into cold, lifeless phenomena. It is a sad thing, but a happenstance that we will each experience personally. Once again, I can describe the how, the where, and the when, but I can not tell you why. If the truth be known, nobody can - not your priest, not your rabbi, not your preacher. They have been trying for centuries. They are all guessing. No matter how confident they may seem, it is all conjecture. No one knows why. Maybe there is no why. In fact, there is no science that deals with the why of anything. We don't know why the tree, the bug, the ant, the human, the universe. We can only deal with the how, the when and the where of it all.

Ever since it happened, I promised myself that I would write this story if I ever had the time, the money and, hopefully, the talent. Well, I've found the time and the money; the talent has been elusive. I finally had to give up waiting for it to come and take matters into my own hands.

This story is a description of the time ... my time; the place ... my place, my hometown, my growing up; the events of my life and those of some of my buddies. It is what happened.

I hope you enjoy this book. And strangely enough, I hope that it makes you cry. I hope it makes you laugh also.

This is not a new story. People have been dying for a long, long time; even youngsters like Charlie. You may not be planning for it right at this moment, but your plans

8

could be interrupted - mine also. Death is not something that we like to dwell upon but it does one well to think about it every now and then.

What makes this story unique is that it happened to me and some of my teenage friends. It was an experience that affected all of us, and for the rest of our lives. None of us would ever be the same. Each of us was marked and bound together. The memory of our experience with Charlie that summer would be forever a part of our being. Charlie was one of us. He was one of the guys, one of the old gang. He was our buddy. He wasn't old enough to be dying. But he did and we watched. Charlie said that he didn't know how. He didn't know how to die. We all watched Charlie die and we learned how to do it with grace and style. I can only hope to do it as well myself when my turn comes along.

My Hometown

My hometown, as I remember, was poor and broke.
The streets were a patchwork of potholes and tar,
Three story tenement houses and out front, an old car.

My hometown, as I remember, and it fills me with pride,
Was filled with calloused hands and blue collared shirts,
Not soft palms waiting to be greased and phony smiles
    wearing suits and ties.

My hometown was telephone poles, seesaws and swings.
My hometown was streets full of kids, and be home before
    dark.
My hometown, as I remember, was bowling alleys and
    draft beer.
My hometown, it was tired and it was poor.
My hometown, it was old ... it was weary ... it was sore.
My hometown it was crusty, rye bread and oleo.
My hometown was salt pork, potatoes and stew.
My hometown, as I remember, wasn't very sweet,
It wasn't indoor cats, and walks for dogs.
It wasn't a piece of cake.

My hometown though, as I remember, wasn't all that bad.
My hometown though, as I remember, wasn't all that sad.
My hometown was a bit of a joke, and a good deal of
    smoke,
But never a pig in a poke.

It was true workingman blue,
And they'll spit in your eye if you say that's a lie.

My hometown, as I remember, wasn't shiny fenders, or
   antique cars.
It was more brass rails and poorly lit bars.
Actually, my hometown, as I remember, it was kind of
   nice.
It was somewhat friendly and sort of warm.
But, I think it's gone, that is, my hometown,
... as I remember.

                              Richard Edward Noble

1 Charlie Gets Liberty

"Rich?" my buddy Willie said in a whisper, slipping up next to me at the pool table. "That was Charlie, man."

"Charlie?"

"Charlie Kareckas!"

"What's he doing home from the Navy?"

"He's dying, man. Didn't you hear?"

"Dying? You've got to be kidding?"

"No man! He got some disease from workin' them X-ray machines for the Navy."

"How come he ain't in some Navy hospital or something?"

"He's gone, man. There ain't no cure. So I guess the Navy just let him go and he's back home at his mom and dad's house until he croaks. They called me up to find out where all of us guys were hanging out now. I guess Charlie just sits around the parlor staring out the window and smoking cigarettes. Mr. and Mrs. K don't know what the hell to do, I guess."

"No joke?"

"No joke, man."

I stared down at the pool table as I pretended to be racking up the balls. Chucky was home from the Navy. He was home to die.

Charlie's home, and my home, was a mill town in the northeast corner of the State of Massachusetts. It was thick with people, rough and tumble, down and dirty. It was tough, blue-collar, working, immigrant folk from just about every country in the world. In fact, today it calls itself *The Immigrant City*. There aren't too many places like it in the United States that I have ever seen. I have been all over the United States and I haven't seen anything like it. I'm not saying that Lawrence is or was something great, I'm just saying that it is unique, a one of a kind. Seeing it once, though, would probably be enough for most folks. This is where Chucky and I were raised.

Robert Frost graduated from Lawrence High School which was just one block north of the "Y" (YMCA). I had to tell you all that. It's the only fact that most of us know to brag on in old Lawrence.

Across from the Y was the Common. The Common was a city park. It had a baseball field, and a softball field, a wading pool and played host to many city events. I've since read that one-eyed Big Bill Haywood was there in 1912 for the famous Bread and Roses labor union strike. The largest labor union strike of the era, involving tens of thousands of workers. Supposedly that strike changed labor history and turned things around for the workingmen, women and children in America.

I always thought that it would be interesting to research that strike. Two of my grandparents were there and probably on different sides of the picket lines.

My grandmother on my mother's side was a weaver, and my grandfather on my father's side was a mill foreman at the Arlington Mills on Broadway. My grandmother worked at the Wood Mill.

The Wood Mill was the largest of its kind. It was built, owned and operated by a William Wood. My grandmother, the weaver, was Polish and my grandfather, the foreman, was Irish. My grandfather might have been standing, looking out a fourth floor window, slapping a club into his palm or wielding a shotgun, while staring down onto the street at my Polish grandmother marching and picketing with her newly arrived, poor, immigrant friends.

Growing up, I never heard one word about unions or strikes. I never heard of the Bread and Roses Strike, or Big Bill Haywood, or Elizabeth Gurley Flynn or Mother Jones. Nor did I hear about the deaths of strikers that were caused by the authorities and then blamed on the strike leaders. A little Italian girl by the name of Anna LoPizzo was shot and killed by police and a fifteen year old Syrian boy by the name of John Ramy was bayoneted by the militia and eventually died in a Lawrence hospital. They framed two of the union leaders for the murders. Smiling Joe Ettor and Arturo Giovannitti were in jail for over a year and finally absolved of the trumped up murder charges brought against them by the state.

My friends and I never discussed any of this. The Bread and Roses Strike of 1912 is the most documented labor/management disaster in union history, yet I never heard mention of it in or out of any of my Lawrence school houses. I don't know if the town was ashamed of it, or it was my Catholic, "support the State and keep the peace" education. Maybe there were such hard feelings over it that everyone just refused to talk about it. So there you go - history in action.

Big Bill Haywood stood up on the bandstand at the Common and gave his famous, or infamous, clenched-fist, unity speech. Each finger standing alone was destructible, but once the hand was closed into a fist and united, the fingers could now defend themselves like a club - today's black power salute.

Dwight David Eisenhower appeared in the Common in 1952 on his first run for the presidency. Between

15

Lawrence, Lowell and Haverhill you probably had several million eligible voters. I don't remember Ike being there at the Common. I would have been nine or ten at the time. I could have been there in the crowd for all I know.

"Hey Charlie, you feel like losing a game of pool, do yah?"

I had just walked into the YMCA. The gang from the old Corner had migrated to the lobby at the Y. I didn't even know what the letters YMCA represented. I really didn't care. The important thing was that for fifty cents I was now an associate member of the YMCA. Being an associate member entitled me to complete and unadulterated access to the Y lobby and its multiple and various facilities. This included a free seat in the "peanut gallery" for TV viewing; access to two official-sized pool tables; visiting privileges to the public reading room; and permission to use one of their chess boards, checker boards, or decks of bicycle playing cards. It was really the best deal for a winter quarters that our street gang had ever stumbled upon. A nice warm lobby with all of the above mentioned amenities, plus vending machines that sold hot chocolate, coffee, potato chips, crackers, Coca-Cola and a whole array of other goodies. I don't know which one of the guys had discovered the associate membership to the Y lobby, but this was the berries. This was the closest we had ever come to being treated as adults in our entire career. It was great; coatracks and everything. Just like real people and not street hooligans or roughnecks. That's what my mother used to call me and my buddies ... roughnecks. "Where are you and your roughneck buddies going tonight? Don't let the cops catch you. STAY OUT OF TROUBLE!" Yah, yah, yah.

I heard a familiar voice call out my name, but my quick scoping out of the peanut gallery revealed no recognizable candidates. I proceeded across the lobby and over to one of the pool tables. I put my quarter in the machine apparatus, shoved in the sliding doohickey thing and then started racking up the balls.

The peanut gallery was always dark, so that you could see the TV which was elevated high up on a wall. If you wanted to change the station on the TV, you had to drag one of the folding or straight-backed chairs over, and climb up onto it. Of course, you had better ask the crowd in the peanut gallery before you ever made such an attempt, if you didn't want to get lynched.

I saw a smile spread under the porkpie hat over in the dim, poorly lit corner.

"Well," Charlie said rising up from his chair. "I suppose that this will be embarrassing. It has been so long since I've shot a game of pool."

"Oh my god, will you listen to this? The overseas, international billiards champion of the entire US Fleet and it's going to be embarrassing? Yah right! Don't give me any of that Willie Mosconi hype. I know better."

Charlie was laughing now. By the time he got to the table, I had the balls all racked.

"You break 'em, hustler," I said with a grin.

Charlie picked himself a cue and rolled it around the table. After three or four cue sticks bumped their way over the felt, he grabbed up the last one and laughed.

"That's a good one. You can probably shoot around corners with that sucker."

"Yah, right."

Charlie didn't look like Charlie anymore. His face was all puffed up. He was a little chubby. He wasn't the lean, mean, fighting machine that he was when he had joined the Navy. If Willie hadn't come up to me and pointed him out, I certainly wouldn't have recognized him. He didn't look sickly though. He still pranced like a young colt with his leather healed loafers clicking on the hardwood floor.

He always dressed well; neat and clean, not fancy. Charlie was a sharp looking guy - neat, trim, good looking. He used to slick back his hair and puff a big wave up in the front, as we all did. We all looked like Elvis in those days.

Charlie had been a member of the "corner gang" since the early days. Myself and John Robert Michael McSheehy Sr. were the organizers of the original Corner Gang. We were on our way home from the St. Rita's grammar school in route number four when we got the bright idea.

The "routes" were the organized and patrolled or supervised pathways to our various neighborhood homes, orchestrated and devised by the Good Nuns. The Good Nuns, the Sisters of Notre Dame, had everything under control. The nuns were sweethearts I know, but I still don't think that I had a nun in any grade who was unable to press her own body weight in the gym. I never saw a nun with a tattoo, though. I walked home in route number four because it was the shortest route. It was only one block long, and it ended at Nell's Variety Store. I don't know what brought up the idea of starting a Corner Gang, but we thought that we would like to start one. John Robert Michael McSheehy Sr. thought that starting a gang would be easy.

"Just start hanging around the same place at the same time everyday, and pretty soon you will have a gang," he suggested. I didn't believe it but I always hated going home so I suggested that we give it a try. John Robert Michael McSheehy Sr., commonly known as Jack, was agreeable to the idea. So everyday after school we went into Nell's, got a bag of Granite State Potato Chips in the sealed fresh aluminum bag and a bottle of C & J (Curran and Joyce) Orange Phosphate, or Lime Rickey and we were in business. We would just sit outside on the steps of the store, or on the sidewalk or the steps leading up to the upstairs apartments and just wait. At supper time we would go home and eat quickly and then run right back. I remember thinking at that time that this was the most exciting thing. I couldn't wait to get back to the Corner after supper each day. It was like fishing. How many bites would we get today and then could we hook them?

It was only a matter of weeks before we had a gang. First came Dolan, who lived just around the corner; then Costello, who lived right across the street from St. Rita's; then Cusack, then Comier, then Charlie who also took route four; then Vinnie Whaley; then Mike Torla who was a friend of Jimmy Costello. It wasn't long before there were fifteen or twenty of us out there every afternoon and evening. It wasn't long before we were a part of the local police department's regular routine also.

"Okay, let's move it. Come on, come on. Don't you little bastards have a home to go to, anyway?"

"You know officer, now that you mention it, you look a little like Dolan. You ever spent any time on Hampshire Street, sir? What do you think Dolan?"

"Daddy, daddy, oh please, can I go home with you tonight?"

"Get movin' you little shits. If we have to get out of this cruiser you guys will be in big trouble."

"Yah like what are you gonna do ... arrest us?"

"That's it. Let's get 'em Billy."

"ALL RIGHT! They're gonna arrest us! SHOTGUN!"

"No no, I'm riding shotgun. You got to ride shotgun last time."

The cops were a regular thing. It was a joke. This was a Catholic tenement-house city, with ten damn kids on every floor. The Police didn't know what to do with us. They tried to keep us moving from one place or from one corner to another. But whatever corner we migrated to, the neighbors didn't want us there either. But the truth was that most of the cops were just like us. They were Irish

19

Catholic or sons of immigrants. They each had six or seven brothers and sisters, and they grew up in the streets or hanging out on the street corners just like we were. They mostly just laughed at us and told us to take a walk and give the poor people living in the surrounding tenement houses a break. We used to go on walks all over the neighborhood, but invariably ended right back where we started; sitting on the steps at Nell's Variety.

"So, what's the deal, you out of the Navy for good now, or just home on leave or something?" Small talk. I knew all the answers but you have to say something.

"I'm gonna be around for awhile," Charlie offered, while inspecting the pool table for a good shot.

"Lucky us."

"Yah, lucky you guys."

The guys who hung out on the Corner were more like family than acquaintances or even buddies. We all knew one another better than we knew our own family members. We sat there everyday, day after day, talking our personal stuff and our personal problems.

Charlie wasn't one to be confessing a lot of personal stuff. He was busy, busy, busy. He was always just coming or just going. He was a year or two older than me and Jack and some of the others. He liked playing cards, shooting pool, and pitching pennies. He was a listener, and a laugher. He was the tease-ee rather than the tease-er. He loved getting razzed, or being the subject of a joke, but he never told any himself, and he didn't tease others. He was the kind of kid who beamed when you called out his name or bumped into him someplace downtown. He loved to be recognized. He loved being a part of the Corner Gang. He played in all of the activities. He was an independent type. He had his own car when we got bigger.

He had his own cigarettes. He never bummed a cigarette. And he didn't indulge those who did. He always had his own money. He never talked or complained about his mother or father or his sisters or brothers. In fact, I don't know if he had a sister. I know he had a younger brother.

Charlie was up the Corner all the time, he was one of the guys. He skipped out of the senior prom to come down to Walter's Variety to get a pack of cigarettes. Walter's was one corner up from Nell's and it was our latest refuge and hangout. Everybody loved that one. A dapper dude in a tux, smoking a cigarette, and reading comic books at Walter's Variety on senior prom night. Walter loved it. He thought that was the greatest. Charlie was a pisser. He was no class clown, but he did unexpected things. Charlie was really so straight and conventional that when he did something out of the ordinary, it really stood out and made you giggle. When you were with Charlie, you always did the talking. I don't ever remember Charlie voicing an opinion on anything. He was easy to be with. He was easy to be around. He was very easy to like. It would not be easy to watch him die.

2   The YMCA

We, in the gang, had grown up on the street corners of Lawrence. We started out at Nell's. Then, for a period, we migrated down the street to Costello's house; then back to Nell's; then to Walter's Variety; then up to the old Howard Playstead; then downtown to the YMCA. The YMCA lobby was the last hangout prior to maturity and the regular evolution to eateries and barrooms and everybody's favorite, the Tally-Ho.

The Y was a strange place, filled with strange people. I don't know why writers remember all the strange people in their lives. You just never seem to read a story in literature about my perfectly normal, everyday type, just a regular, average guy, Uncle Joe. It just doesn't happen. Maybe there really aren't any just regular people in the world. They only seem regular if you don't really know them. Once you get to know them they take on all the qualities of the unusual.

The Y had John the Thinker, Harry the Walker, Mister America, General Mills, Beenie the Baseball Card Genius; Cartsie and Hannagan - the sado-masochist Abbot and Costello, Popeye, Fat George - the dirty joke lexicon; Vinnie the Ginny - a Mafioso type who would bet on anything - and the list goes on and on.

John the Thinker was a rather sad case. He was from the peripatetic school. He paced all over the place, back and forth about the lobby, talking out loud to himself. The conversation never stopped. But if somebody walked by and said, "How's it going John?" John would immediately respond. If you asked him a question, he would answer appropriately. Everybody tried to eavesdrop on John to find out what the hell he was talking about, or who he was talking to. But nobody could ever figure it out. Some nights John would really get into it. He would get real animated. Once in awhile he would even burst out with a yell ... "NO! YOU CAN'T MAKE ME DO IT!" Momentarily everybody would stop whatever they were doing and look over at John. We all wanted to hear that key phrase, the Rosetta stone of the John the Thinker inner being. Like, "NO, I WON'T DO IT! I WON'T GIVE YOU BASTARDS THE SECRET TO THE ATOMIC BOMB. NEVER! NEVER! NEVER!" The whole Y would hush over for a couple of seconds and stare over at John in heated anticipation, but nothing would ever come of it. John would just roll on and return to a quieter tone. Most everybody would just shrug their shoulders, or shake their heads in disappointment. Oh well, maybe next time.

One time a bunch of us were riding across town and we saw John the Thinker in his wool, pullover, knitted hat giving a sidewalk lecture to the usual crowd of none. Somebody rolled down a window and screamed out "HEY JOHN!" Poor John nearly took a crap in his hat. First he leaped about four feet into the air, and then he ran into a doorway to hide. Well, no one could figure it, so naturally they had to try it a few more times. Each time we passed John, somebody would yell, and poor John would throw a conniption.

John was obviously shell shocked or suffering from something from the war. Most of us didn't like the "make

John jump" tactic, but there was always one. No matter what we did to the culprit - punch his arms until they were black and blue; hit him on the head several hundred times with newspapers or rolled up magazines, or bare knuckles - "nuggies"; or throw him out of the car - one nitwit would always spot John on the street somewhere and give a yell. I can still see John leaping behind a pillar downtown, or ducking into a doorway, or just covering his head and hitting the dirt. I still feel ashamed about it, but whenever we get together and somebody mentions John the Thinker, it's spit up laughter time. It is sad, man. I'm sorry, it is just sad.

Harry the Walker was everywhere. It all started out very innocently. A couple of my buddies and I were standing on a corner somewhere and along comes Harry the Walker. "Wasn't that Harry?" somebody asks. "Yah, I wonder what he is doing way over here?"

No big deal, but, from then on, we start to see Harry the Walker everywhere. He is like Alfred Hitchcock. He just keeps popping up in every scene. We see him up at the library at Merrimack College. We see him across town at the Andover Book Store. We go for a walk in the woods, and there's Harry with a backpack. Who would believe it? The clincher was one day we go to the big city, Boston. We go riding around on the subway. We don't know where we are. We are totally lost. We're in this underground somewhere. We are under some big overpass. We spot this Joe and Nemo's hot dogs and cafeteria across the street. We figure we'll go get a hot dog and get our bearings. We get inside and there's a waiting line. We get in the line and start figurin' our hot dog. I decide to ask somebody where the heck we are. I tap the guy in front of me on the shoulder. He turns around and, you guessed it, it's Harry. "Harry, where the hell are we?"

"No problem, no problem. You go down here a block and you take a left, then go two blocks and hang a right. How you guys doin' anyway?"

"Good Harry, good."

In any case, we follow Harry's directions and we're on the train back to Lawrence. We start wondering what Harry was doing at Joe and Nemo's in the middle of the underground in downtown nowhere, Boston. But then we said to ourselves, Harry didn't ask what the hell we were doing at Joe and Nemo's. Why should we be wondering why he was there? So we get back over to the Lawrence train station and we take a walk over to the Y. We walk into the peanut gallery, and who is sitting in the front row, center?

"Harry? How the hell are yah?"

"Good guys. Real good. How did you like your Joe and Nemo's hot dog?"

"We loved it Harry, just loved it. How was yours?"

"Good, great. I love Joe and Nemo's hot dogs. They're the best. How you guys doin' anyway?"

"Great Harry, great."

We made jokes from then on about Harry's ubiquitousness. Somebody would say that one day they would like to climb the Matterhorn, and we'd all say. Naw, don't bother. You get all the way to the top and Harry will be sitting there sucking on a Popsicle. "How you doin' guys; how you doin'?" Wouldn't you like to be the first man on the moon? What the hell for. You get there and there's Harry walking by carrying an American flag. "How you doin' guys. How you doin'?"

One day three of us went to Philadelphia. We were standing out in front of the Liberty Bell. A man walked by with his collar rolled up and wearing a ball cap just like Harry's. "How you doin' guys; how you doin'?"

We all said, "Good Harry, good." Then we realized where we were. We chased all over town trying to find Harry but we couldn't. We all swear to this day that it was Harry. The next time we saw Harry at the Y we asked him. "Were you in Philadelphia last week, Harry?"

"Sure I was," he said with a grin. "I'm everywhere. You never know when you're going to bump into Harry. How you guys doin' anyway?"

"Good Harry, good."

Beenie the Baseball Card Genius was a funny case. He didn't look retarded or anything like that. He was just sort of really, really stupid. He constantly said stupid things. You couldn't really have a conversation with him. It was just ridiculous. He always laughed at the wrong places, or said something that let you know instantly that he wasn't listening. I really think that he just liked to have people talk to him. He was so happy when somebody spoke to him that he didn't even listen to what they said. Just the fact that they spoke was thrill enough. But if you asked him to give you the stats on Ted Williams, or Mickey Mantle or somebody, anybody in any sport, he would start rattling off like some computer. So if Beenie was standing outside the door at the Y as you walked in, you would say, "Beenie, 1938 world series?" And zip, zip, zip, Beenie would start rattling off the facts. So then you would laugh, pat Beenie on the shoulder and go rambling on your way.

If fat George was there, he would always have a crowd around him in some dark corner and he would be telling his zingers. He had a memory for dirty jokes that just never quit. He could go on for days and never tell the same joke twice.

Mister America was unique to say the least. Everybody has a story here in the naked city, and Mister America's story was this.

One time when he was a kid, he spent months working on a model ship. When he finally got it finished, he showed it to his dad. His dad took one look at it; saw a flaw in it, and threw it on the floor.

"It ain't perfect son. I don't want anything around here that ain't perfect."

That story always made me laugh. Like there was something in Lawrence somewhere that was perfect? Come on! In any case, Mister America became a bodybuilder and weightlifter. He won the Mister Boston contest a couple of times, and the Mister New England championship. Supposedly he had been asked to play the part that Steve Reeves got in the movie Samson, or Ulysses or something.

Mister America was really a masterpiece, though. No fooling. He was ahead of his time. He had arms on him, the size of a man's thighs. He was a super bodybuilder. There was really nothing like him in those days. He was one of a kind. He made Steve Reeves look like junior league. He used to work out with the wannabes downstairs, but he was always getting into trouble and pissing off Popeye.

Popeye was one of the YMCA directors, or whatever they were called. He worked behind the main desk. He looked just like Popeye the cartoon character. He was mostly bald with a couple of sprigs of hair standing up on the top of his head. He worked out with weights all his life but he was older. He was still muscular but yet wrinkly. He, like Popeye the cartoon character, had big biceps that popped up when he flexed his arms, but no triceps. Everybody called him Popeye, even to his face. That was his name, Popeye. It didn't seem to bother him - especially when people would say "Mister" Popeye.

"Mister Popeye, sir, could we get a deck of playing cards?"

"Sure boys, sure. Here you go."

"Thank you, Mister Popeye."

Popeye was almost unflappable. The only person that ever got him upset was Mister America.

Mister America didn't work. He couldn't. It messed up the contour of his muscles or something. I have no idea what he did for a living. Nobody did. He was always down the Y, either working out or watching TV in the peanut gallery.

He was a real good looking guy. He looked like a movie star - hence the story about his almost movie career. But he did strange things. He is the only person in history that Popeye ever suspended from the Y. He got suspended a number of times. The first time was on ladies night.

Once a week the YWCA got the use of some of the facilities - the basketball court, the swimming pool, one of the gyms and the shower room. Well, Mister America had removed a couple of bricks in the wall of the men's weight room and was selling peeks into the shower room when the ladies were washing up. What really made this nearly impossible to believe was the women who used the facilities; these were old women, no teenagers in this crowd. These were grey-haired, old women; heavy weights, who lived at the YW across the street and worked in the greasy-spoons down on Essex Street. If Popeye had just let those girls go get Mister America, they would have knocked the hell out of him. He would have been in big trouble.

The next big problem Popeye had was somebody kept "dumping a load" on the concrete floor of the men's shower room. Of course, no hourly wage employees would clean it up, so Popeye himself had to do it. This went on for a good while. Finally Popeye came in on Mister America, and caught him right in the act. Popeye ordered Mister America to clean it up. Mister America actually did it. Then Popeye suspended him indefinitely. Mister

America was down everyday begging for his rights to be returned. Finally Popeye allowed Mister America an associate membership, but that was it. Mister America could sit in the lobby and watch the TV. He shot pool once in awhile, but he was so damn big, he could barely hold the stick properly. One time he did a break for a game of Eight Ball that nearly sent the cue ball through the wall. That almost caused him to lose his tentative associate membership.

Well, as hard as this all seemed to believe, old Charlie was becoming one of the regular Y guys. I was in my last year of high school, so I was there everyday after school and early on Saturday and Sunday mornings. Whenever I would come in, Charlie would already be there or would be coming in the door behind me. Sometimes when I came in, I would go up to Popeye to get some change or the checkerboard or something. I would look down the small corridor that led to the men's room, and there Charlie would be playing chess with John the Thinker, or checkers with Harry the Walker, or Forty-fives with Mister America. He was now on regular speaking terms with all of them. All of us corner guys would laugh. It just seemed funny. But Charlie had found a home away from home. We asked him if he could figure out who John the Thinker was always mumbling to, or what he was talking about, but he couldn't. He said that John seemed to have invented his own language. He said that he really didn't think that there was anything funny about any of the Y guys. Once you got to know them, they were just like everybody else, he claimed.

Yah right! Mister America was just a regular guy? Come on now Charlie? Charlie even got to know all of their real names. Now that was really funny. Charlie would come walking into the lobby, pass by Mister America, and say, "Hey, how you doin' today, Hubert?"

Hubert? Oh my god! I had the very strong feeling that if I ever called Mister America "Hubert" my body parts would be found floating somewhere down the Merrimack River, or in one of the industrial canals.

Oh yah, Lawrence was the "Venice" of the Industrial Northeast. We had this canal system all over the valley. The mill owners had built them way back in the 1840's. These canals were a little different than your regular waterways though. They had some real strange sea creatures growing in there. As kids we used to think that they were some kind of prehistoric fish, but today I know better. Those suckers were man made. That's for sure.

Charlie always checked the peanut gallery whenever he was leaving or going anywhere. Charlie was always on his way to somewhere. I ended up going with him lots of times on his errands or runs about town.

What did we talk about? Nothing really, mostly about stuff that was on TV last night. You know; Did you see that guy who ate his own foot on the Ed Sullivan show last night? Or did you watch Sid Caesar playing meat in his rock and roll band? We didn't get metaphysical, or even philosophical. We just hung out together. That's what all of us guys did. We just hung out. We talked if we wanted, or we didn't talk if we didn't want to.

When I went with Charlie he always had urgent things to do that really weren't urgent. We would go down to Pappy's Bakery on Common Street for example. Charlie would pick up a couple of loaves of Italian bread. I would go in with him and get me a small sandwich torpedo roll. The ethnic breads in Lawrence were unbelievable. You didn't need any butter, jelly or peanut butter - just a chunk of bread. I'd sit there and eat my bread. I used to like to break off some crust and then dig out all of the insides. All the doughy, gooey delicious yeast flavored dough. Then when I had nothing but crust left, I'd crunch that down.

When Charlie and I and some of the other guys were coming home from one of the Central Catholic High School basketball games, we would all stop at the Polish bakery on Exchange Street. The bread would just be coming out of the oven at that time. We would all get a loaf of bread or a half a dozen bulkie rolls. Can you imagine being a kid and just eating a whole loaf of Polish light rye as a treat? It seems funny now. But it was no joke. That bread was so good! It was better than an éclair or a jelly donut. They had jelly donuts right there too, but nobody ever got one. Everybody would be walking home on those cold winter nights digging our mitts into the warm, doughy, stuffing of a loaf of Polish rye.

Sometimes Charlie would take the bread, or the pizza or whatever over to his house. Sometimes I would go upstairs with him. Whatever he brought would surprise his mom and dad; Oh look what Charlie brought, some delicious Italian bread, or some French bread, or whatever.

After a few times, I stopped going upstairs with Charlie because of the look in his mom and dad's eyes. It was sad. They were always on the edge of a tear. There was no hiding it. You could just feel the confusion in their eyes. It was obvious that they just loved me or any of the guys. Because now Charlie had somebody other than them, and they were useless and they knew it. Every time they looked at him, they just wanted to grab onto him and bawl their eyes out. You just knew it. It didn't take a whole lot of perception and understanding, or empathy. It was obvious. Sometimes Charlie would look at them, then over to me and wink. I would nod my head and we'd both laugh or grin like we had some kind of a secret. What the secret was, I still haven't figured out, but we had something. You tell me.

I would only go upstairs if Charlie insisted, and sometimes he did. "Come on Rich. I know you can take it." Then we would both laugh as we got out of the car and went upstairs to greet the desperate duo. Believe me, I felt for those two. But what's to say? Like Tonto of Lone Ranger fame used to say; Me know nothing.

Sometimes we went to the Post Office on the corner of Broadway and Essex to pick up the mail. Sometimes we would go over to Bea's Sandwich Shop up on Broadway and get a cutlet or a B-B-Q. Or down to Lawton's by the Sea for a couple of Essem hot dogs on a hot bun, grilled with butter.

Lawton's was on one of the canals so that's how it became Lawton's by the Sea. And, "Yes 'em, it's Essem, the finest hot dog in the land." That was a jingle that you heard all over the radio. You couldn't give away a Hebrew National or anything else in Lawrence. It was Essem hot dogs, Essem Polish kielbasy, Essem baloney. And you washed down your baloney with a Holihan's Black Horse Ale right from the local Holihan's Brewery. Everybody said that it was the river water from the Merrimack that made the difference. That was a joke, of course. But the Merrimack was the source of Lawrence's drinking water. It was so polluted that they used every purification technique known to mankind at the time to make it potable. Scientists came from all over the world just to take a tour of the Lawrence reservoir and city water purifying system.

One late Friday afternoon Charlie came zooming into the Y lobby. He peeked around the corner and into the peanut gallery. He saw me sitting there and invited me to accompany him on his rounds. We buzzed around here and there. We hit the Lawrence Library across from St. Mary's Church. Chucky's mom was working there as a volunteer on Fridays. Chuck goes in to say hello or something and when he came out he said he was going to run into the Church for a quick confession.

I had been raised Catholic. Charlie and I were both altar boys together at St. Rita's School and at the Immaculate Conception Church. I was finishing up, right now, at Central Catholic. But at this point in my career, I was not overly interested in religion. I was very unhappy with God. So far he had killed my cat, Blackie; my only puppy dog ever, Rex; my best and most loved Uncle Joe, and a few short years ago, my father.

I stood there right in the kitchen watching my dad die. I watched his chest heaving up and down as he tried gulping in the air. But puff-puff, huff-huff and two minutes later he was dead. God kills everybody, I felt.

But I wasn't afraid of God either. Why not go inside St. Mary's while Charlie told all of his terrible sins to the good Father. Charlie had sins on his soul? Come on, get real!

I went inside with Charlie. There was always a quiet, peacefulness inside St. Mary's Church. I took up a seat in the last pew while Charlie went clicking his heels over to Father Kelly's stall.

Father Kelly was the kind of priest who could forgive anything. The only penalty he ever gave was three Our Fathers and three Hail Marys.

"Bless me Father, for I have sinned. I just raped and killed my mother. I then dissolved her body in acid and poured it into the Reservoir."

"Are you sorry, my son?"

"Sure I'm sorry. I should have dumped it into one of the canals and not the Reservoir where it might pollute the drinking water system."

"Very good my son, you will never do that again, will you?"

"No Father. I have no need to. She won't be coming back."

"Very good, my son, now say a good Act of Contrition and for your penance say three Our Fathers and three Hail Marys."

"Oh my God, I am "hardly" sorry for having offended Thee."

As I sat there in the last pew in the last row, I thought about Charlie. He was a regular guy. He knew the score. He couldn't really believe all of this religion stuff, could he? But then again what did I know? Charlie was really on the yellow brick road to Doomsville. It wasn't going to be too long from now, either. I wasn't going to be the judge. Who wouldn't want to go to heaven if there really was such a thing? So, you have to get humble and say a few Our Fathers and a few Hail Marys - kiss a little butt. What good is it trying to be a hero, if you only end up in hell for it anyway? He was doing the smart thing. Just like that thief who was nailed on the cross next to Jesus. He lived a life of crime and debauchery but at the last moment he says, "Hey man, you look like God to me."

"My Father will remember you, good buddy."

So off to heaven he goes. Hey, why not?

While Charlie was waiting in Father Kelly's line, Father Casey came strolling out of his station and sat down next to me.

"Are you waiting to go to confession, my son?"

"No Father, but thanks anyway."

"Well, you know my son, even if you have no sins you can go to confession and receive extra grace."

Business was obviously slow, tonight. Father Kelly always had a waiting line. The three other priests just sat in their stalls waiting for the race to begin, chomping at the bit.

Father Casey obviously didn't remember me. I had quit the altar boys when he took over. I never liked him. He told me nobody quits Jesus. I was only in the fifth grade at the time, but I told him it had nothing to do with Jesus. I loved Jesus. I just didn't care for him. He poked his index finger into my chest and told me to be there that coming Sunday if I knew what was good for me. When I didn't show, I never heard from him again.

He also showed up two hours late for my dad's DEATH! My mother and sister actually called a priest before they called the doctor. They thought that saving my dad's soul was more important than saving his body. The doctor arrived after my father died and Father Casey arrived even after that. When he found out that my father was already dead, he was about to turn around and leave. My mother and sister nearly threw a fit.

"What about the Last Rites?" they both screamed.

"Oh yah," he says, "definitely. You know the soul often doesn't leave the body until hours after the person has died."

Yah right, I said to myself. Nice save Father Casey. He could fool those two, but I wasn't biting, even then. Souls, spirits, angels, devils - Voo-doo, man! Voo-doo!

But what was I going to do now? Father Casey was eager to lay some extra grace on me. I could just tell him no, but why be mean about all of this hooey.

"Would you like to step into the confessional, my son? I would be more than happy to listen to your sins."

The man was really desperate. He would even hear some old sins. I suppose that I could make some up. What difference did it make? I used to have a regular routine. But I was too big to be telling about having impure thoughts. What if he asks what kind of impure thoughts? Then what do I do? Describe all my fantasies to him? No no, I can't go in there and make up sins. But why couldn't

I just tell him some easy sins like eating meat on Friday. Man, they didn't even have that one anymore. All those poor suckers stuck in hell because of a ham sandwich. What happened to them? They all get a "get out of jail free" card or what? Voo-doo! Pure Voo-doo! How about taking the Lord's name in vain? I could lay that one on him. Oh forget it, I told myself. I'll make up some stuff. The poor guy didn't know what to do with himself.

"O.K. Father. I'll earn some extra grace."

He was pretty happy about the whole deal. He got up and rushed into his cubicle. I sat there in my pew for about thirty seconds. I almost had my spiel all set.

"Hey Rich? You ready to go?" It was Charlie.

"Yah. You all done?"

"Sure, it don't take me long these days. I don't do anything."

"I wonder why. O.K., let's get out of here."

As we scooted past the confessional and headed for the big door at the back of the church, I could hear Father Casey climbing out of his box; "Where the heck is that guy?" he was probably asking himself.

On the road to perdition, pops - on the road to perdition.

3   The Cottage

Charlie was home. Home on "Liberty." He was granted the liberty to die. I was only eighteen but I had already seen more of death than I had wanted. It wasn't fair. But what is fair? None of us asked to be here. What's fair about that? It is one thing to hear about people dying or to even have people that you know die. The problem comes with watching people die who you really care about. That hurts. Of course, if your feelings are shallow to begin with or if you never let yourself really care about anybody, you have no problem. Death really doesn't seem to bother some people until it is right on top of them.

Charlie was finding a life. He had adopted the Y and, of course, he had all of his old buddies, the gang from the Corner. Sometimes you would forget about Charlie being sentenced to death row, but it was never far from the surface. Every now and then he would be into the hospital for a day or two. I still don't know what Leukemia is. It has something to do with red and white blood cells. You need a balance. If one keeps eating the other one or too many of one kind grow to overpower the other kind, you die. Our own bodies seem to be in a constant battle between life and death. Some things inside of us are trying to keep us alive and others things right inside our own bodies are trying to kill us. It's crazy.

Everybody says that life is a miracle. It's no miracle. It's a catastrophe. It's a Rube Goldberg world created by an insane Doctor Frankenstein. So really, I guess, Charlie was nothing new. Just more fodder for God's cannons.

This lightning was striking too close for me. I didn't like it. I wanted to strike out and fight back, but who do I attack?

Why am I alive? - Answer; You are alive to know, love and serve God in this world and in the next.

Wow, sounds like something out of a Marine Corps manual. What's to know? Who's to love? And after you have seen a little bit of this world, who in their right mind would want to see the next one?

Every year since I was probably fourteen or fifteen the gang somehow finagled a summer cottage at the beach. We would get somebody older to talk to the realtor; or one of the older looking guys would just lie about his age. The first cottage that we rented took about thirty investors. We all chipped in ten or twenty bucks. We slept on the beds, on the floors, in the kitchen, in our cars out in front in the parking spaces, wherever. It was a real disaster. The cottage was called the Marilyn. We created such a disturbance in the neighborhood, that the police finally put a condemned sign on the door and wouldn't let any of us back inside. We weren't even allowed back in to get any clothes or bedding that we had brought. We thought that we were going to get sued or something. But since nobody had any real names, and because the landlord had overcharged us considerably in the first place, everybody was just happy to see us get lost.

As time went by we did a little better. We limited membership to twelve or so. Eventually we rented a cottage at Salisbury Beach from a middle aged guy who was a rather strange dude himself.

The cottage was a duplex. The owner rented out one side to us and left the other side open for his personal excursions. He was always cheating on his wife and he needed a place to bring his conquests. It also provided a good excuse for him when he just wanted to get out by himself. "Hey Honey, I've got some work to do on the cottage this weekend." - Or "I think I'll take a little ride to the beach and make sure everything is all right at the cottage." He would often have a few beers at our place and ogle all the little girls we had visiting.

As we got a little older, we each put up more money and got fewer guys. Sometimes the whole gang would rent two or three different places.

It was getting to be about that time. We had to start taking names and collecting money. We were going to get the duplex again this year. It was a nice place about two blocks down from the beach. But who really cared about the beach. All we did was drink beer and party. We would send scouts down to the water's edge every now and then to bring back girls. We made jokes about paving the beach over and pulling the plug on all the cold, salty water. It was a wild time. We loved it.

We were sitting in the peanut gallery one evening. Willie, Jack, Dutch, myself and a couple of others, had the quota nearly filled on our seashore paradise.

"We got one more bed open," Willie said. "Who do you think we can sucker into buying the last spot?" We all laughed.

"I'll take it," Charlie said.

We were all a little shocked to say the least. Our summer cottage at the beach was not a retreat, no rosary beads or Bibles allowed. This was sin city, if it was at all possible. It was booze and beer, and girls, and drunk and dirt and PARTY! We were all so young and crazy; I can't even believe it today. But everybody goes through it, I guess. We had our turn and we were looking forward to it once again.

"How much do you need?" Charlie said standing up and pulling out his wallet.

Nobody answered. We were all sitting there looking at Charlie. He had never been in on one of our cottage deals. He had joined the Navy right after high school. He had heard about some of our summer time adventures though. He certainly had to know what we were up to.

"Ah Charlie, you know, the cottage ... well it's ... well it can get a little raunchy ... I mean ..."

"I know. How much?"

"We're all chipping in a hundred bucks each? Then every weekend we all throw in twenty bucks apiece for booze and steaks and burgers and dogs and stuff for the grill. Any damages to the place, we all split it at the end of the season."

"Oh, you guys eat when you are at the beach? I thought that it was just all booze," Charlie said, incredulously.

"Hell no, we eat. What do you think we are - animals?"

Charlie counted out a hundred dollars and handed it to Willie. Willie didn't know if he should take it or not. He looked at the rest of us sitting there in the peanut gallery. One by one we each shrugged our shoulders approvingly.

"Okeydokey," Willie said with a grin, snatching up Charlie's hundred. "You're in, and ... ah, may God have mercy on your soul." Charlie just shook his head and grinned and we all laughed like hell.

"He's kidding Charlie. We don't do anything. There's nobody here who still ain't a virgin," Jack said.

"Hey, you speak for yourself, buddy."

42

"Oh come on?" Jack said. "Who have you had sex with lately?"

"None of your business, man. Besides don't you ever talk to your sister?"

"Oh come on! If you had sex with my sister, good luck to you, man."

"O.K., I've got to get going. I'll see you guys later."

"Yah, O.K. Charlie, we'll see you later."

After Charlie left, we all just sat there looking at one another. We were all thinking the same thing - was this really a good idea?

"Man, did we just blow it?"

"I don't know. I suppose we could all live like human beings for one summer for Charlie's sake."

"Not me!" Jack said. "I don't want to be no human being." Everybody started laughing. "Besides, we would have to sign up for an instruction course or something. Which one of you clowns knows how to be a human being?"

"You've got a good point there."

"No seriously," Jack went on. "Charlie is a big boy. He's been in the Navy for a couple or three years. They're not exactly a bunch of angels in there. Besides we ain't all that bad. What do we do? Drink a couple of beers? Have a little party? What the hell?"

"What do we do? My god! What about the Marilyn getting condemned? What about the brawling in the parking lot? What about the police raiding us and you throwing Nancy Sullivan over the fence and into the swamp? What about Niki running around nude? What about Cartsie and Hannagan having naked street races, what about ..."

"Oh hell, that was nothing."

"And speaking about angels, what about Charlie? I don't want to see the guy go to hell because of us."

43

"Why? You got plans of going someplace else?"

"It don't matter where I'm going. I just don't want to take nobody with me."

4   Helping Charlie

I didn't really have my mind made up on hell yet either.

"How could we be responsible for Charlie going to hell? We don't tell Charlie what to think? We don't tell Charlie what to do? We don't tell Charlie, anything. If he wants to be good, he can be good. If he wants to be bad, he can be bad. That's his business."

"True, but why make it hard for the guy? Why put his butt in the middle of it all?"

"In the middle of what?"

"Like Jack said, what do we do that's so bad? Drink a few beers? Have a little fun? We ain't out killing nobody. Come on."

We rented the cottage from our buddy, the Pervert, once again. He threw in the months of June and September as a bonus. Both those months were usually too cold for the beach, but what did that have to do with us? Who needs a beach?

School was out. I had graduated. I didn't have a fulltime job yet. I was sitting down at the Y in the peanut gallery when Charlie came zipping in.

"Hey Rich, want to go to the beach?"

"Sure, but ain't you rushing it a little? This is only Tuesday. Weekend don't start until Friday."

"Well, my folks are moving into their summer cottage over at Hampton, so I might as well be there, as here."

"Okay, sounds good to me."

"You got to go home and get some stuff?"

"I suppose I had better."

Charlie took me over to my house. I ran in and told the Old Lady what I was up to, and came running out. When I climbed into Charlie's car he just looked at me. I had my bathing suit in one hand and my towel in the other.

"That's it?" Charlie said with a smirk.

"What? What do you need to go to the beach?"

"Some sheets and a blanket maybe - a tooth brush?"

"I don't use a bed, man. I usually just drink until I pass out. Wherever I wake up, that's good enough for me, and I gargle."

"If you say so."

So, it was off to the beach for a summer with Charlie. This should be fun - if not fun ... different.

It was Friday before I knew it and the guys were starting to roll in for the weekend. Charlie had to go over to Hampton to his mother's for supper. I was sitting in a chair that I had leaned up against the stairwell, when the boys came packing in. They all stopped dead in the doorway. They looked around the cottage. It was clean. They had never seen it in that condition before. Nobody said anything though. They just stared, dumbly.

"Where's Charlie?"

"He's having supper over at his mother's in Hampton."

"You've been down here all week with him?"

"Yah."

There was a silence.

"Well?"

"Well what?"

"Everything going okay?"

"Yah."

46

"What you been doing?"

"What have I been doing?"

"Yah, what you been doin'?"

"You mean after we cleaned and scrubbed the upstairs' bedrooms; went to the store and bought sheets and pillow cases; made all the beds - military style, with square corners. Did you ever bounce a half dollar off your bed?"

"No."

"Well, knock yourselves out. Run upstairs and bang a few around."

"Looks like you've been busy down here too."

"Does it? Why? I can't really understand it. All we did was scrub and clean everything visible or invisible. Swab all the decks. Scrub down and dust and wax all the furniture ..."

"You waxed the furniture? That seems like a waste of good effort, time and money. Everything in here is late period garbage dump. The Pervert doesn't put anything worth a nickel in here. He knows we're coming. He ain't stupid."

"Well stupid or not, he's got a new commode in the toilet and new curtains..."

"Curtains?"

"Wait a minute, wait a minute! Let me finish; a magazine rack, cigarette trays, a plunger..."

"Wow! A plunger? I like that."

"... and toilet paper."

"What? Charlie doesn't like the Eagle Tribune?"

"No Tribune for Charlie. No no no."

"Take a look inside the fridgerator."

Jack went over to the fridgerator. He had a troop of little elves right at his heels. He opened the fridge door.

"Wow! My favorite, little ugly Kruger bottles."

"Forget the beer. Look at the   ."

"What? I'm lookin'"

"You don't see anything?"

"What's to see?"

"Ohhhh, God! ... You don't notice the absence of any blood stains, human puke, pubic hair, jockey shorts, panties and whatever that white, sticky stuff was? What the heck was that anyway?"

"Oh come on? You're kidding us?"

"Well, it was white and hard and sticky ..."

"Dried milk, man. It was probably dried milk."

"MILK? Who ever brought milk into this place? You trying to tell me we had somebody here last year eating Wheaties?"

"No, no, we were on that White Russian kick for awhile."

"White Russians? Phew, that makes me feel better. I couldn't believe that anybody would ..."

"Well, stranger things have happened around here, man. Remember that debutante we found sleeping behind the refrigerator one Monday morning?"

"Boy, I don't really know if I want to sleep on a sheet," Dutch groaned.

"It ain't really that bad, Dutch. Don't you have sheets at home?"

"Of course I have sheets at home. But if I wanted sheets, I could have stayed at home this summer and saved a hundred bucks."

"Yah, but you wouldn't have the beach."

"There's a beach here? You're kidding? Where?"

"Just go back out the front door. Walk down one block. Hang a left and go straight until your feet hit water."

"You told me that same story last year, and I ended up standing in a puddle out in front of a rotisserie chicken joint."

"That's because you went to the corner and took a RIGHT. I said take a left."

"Ohhhh? I'll try it again sometime."

"Do you want to go now?"

"No. No rush. I'll try it sometime this season. Take a right you said?"

"A left! A LEFT!"

"Okay, okay, don't get all bent out of shape over it. I got ya."

"So after you cleaned the upstairs and the downstairs and put in the new commode and got the white sticky stuff out of the fridge ... anything else?"

"Well, nothing much; we just pretty much done what any of you guys would have done. We went and bought a squeegee and a bucket and washed all the windows and then ..."

"No? Come on?"

"Take a look man? Squeegee clean. Look for yourself - upstairs in the bedroom too. I had to sit Charlie up on my shoulders to get the window in the toilet on the outside."

The guys had enough of my tales of a week with Charlie, but I had more to tell, and I wasn't about to let up. Dutch was really the one who seemed most upset. He had taken up bodybuilding a few years ago. He had become kind of chummy with Mister America at the Y. He had developed some bodybuilder habits. He liked to drink cold pork and beans right out of the can; or eat a whole can of Spam wrapped in one slice of white bread; or drink a jar of honey; or eat a one pound package of cream cheese and wash it down with a quart of buttermilk. Part of bodybuilding seems to be seeing what kind of abuse your body will take, both on the outside and on the inside.

"So then we went down and talked with "Pete" down at the hardware store ..."

"Pete?"

"Oh yah, Pete Habeeb; he owns the hardware and his family owns Habeeb Bar and Grill down on Common Street."

"Oh really?"

"They have two daughters, Helen and Annita."

"Annita Habeeb? Are you sure? I don't know any A-rabs named Annita."

"Annita, Addida, Abdulla ... who cares."

"Well, if you are going to give me the whole story of you and Charlie at the seashore, I want it accurate, man."

"Why?"

"Hey, you never know, maybe one day I'll write a book."

"Well, leave out the last part and make it a mystery."

"Ha ha ha, so what next?"

"So then after we got the rake and the two garbage cans, we raked up the yard. After that, I figured that we deserved a beer; so I got two ugly little Kruger bottles and Charlie and I sat down out on the stoop out front. Charlie lit up a cigarette. While he was smoking his cigarette, he noticed that the neighborhood was adrift with spent cigarette butts."

"Noooo? I'm so surprised."

"Well, it was, but it ain't now. We F B I-ed the whole thing."

"You F B I-ed it?"

"Yah. That's what Charlie called it. It's one of them Navy terms like 'ship shape' and 'all aboard'. You know 'deck the halls' and all that stuff."

"I don't think so. It ain't F B I, its "police the area" or something like that."

"Who cares? Whatever? The whole neighborhood has been completely F B I-ed. And let me ask you this? You've been coming here to the beach for how many years?"

"All my life."

"Me too. So where's the garbage dump?"

"The garbage dump? I haven't the slightest."

"Well, if you want to go see it sometime, just ask me. I'll take you right over there."

"I'd like to see it," Dutch piped.

"Yah, I knew you would. But for you, it will cost. No free ride. You would probably want to move into the dump and get your money out of this place, and we can't afford it. It is too late now buddy."

Eighteen years living on Chelmsford Street and I hardly knew anybody. One week with Charlie at the beach, and I knew everybody on the road. Everybody wanted to talk with Charlie. I don't know whether it was that constant smile on his face or that funny porkpie hat or what. Me, I was like the invisible man. I'd stand right in front of people and they would walk right over me, but Charlie? Even that jerk with the cigarette as we were F B I-ing the neighborhood. A big fat guy with a beer can in one hand and a butt hanging out of his mouth. He sees Charlie and me clipping along, F B I-ing the whole street, and what does he do? He flicks his butt right out in front of Charlie. I felt like climbing up onto his porch and mushing my fist right into his nose. Charlie runs over with a big grin, crushes the butt and picks it up. Then he tips his hat to the slob. Two days later we're up on this guy's front porch, drinking one of his beers and shooting the breeze about life in general. I really don't get it, but that was Charlie for you. That was Charlie.

5   Niki and the Police

Time flies when you are having fun and everyday was just zooming along. We had earned a new reputation at the Cottage this year. The neighborhood loved us. Everybody now walked by our place and they all smiled and said hello. Last year everybody took the long way around. Certainly no women and children would walk unescorted by any place that we had previously rented. Even when and if they had a male bodyguard, they would cut out to the highway rather than be forced to confront the terrible ten or our dirty dozen. This year it was, 'good morning boys' and 'how you doin' fellas'. My god, we were now fellas and boys instead of gangsters and hoodlums.

One day this lady directly across the way comes over and asks if we will watch her two little kids because she wanted to take a quick run to the grocery store. There were four of us standing around the kitchen in various poses, each with a beer in hand. We were all dumbfounded. We couldn't even speak. After a moment or two Charlie jumped up and said; "Sure Nancy, no problem. Take your time." After the woman left, we all looked at Charlie and said; "Nancy?"

Charlie shrugged, and with a grin answered; "Ah yah, Nancy."

We had Nancy, the hubby and the kids, along with a few other of the neighbors over for B-B-Q ribs one Sunday afternoon. And when everybody was done, they all cleaned everything up and the wives did all of the dishes. We usually left everything in the sink for about a week, then threw it all out and bought new stuff down at the dime store. If any woman walked into our place in the past, she usually started to puke. This was all Chucky's fault.

This was all getting to be rather unbelievable - until Niki finally showed up one Saturday evening.

Niki was the kind of a girl that every teenage boy should have as a part of his memory. Niki was also an A-rab. We had a large Syrian population in Lawrence. I say Syrian because that is what it said on the bakeries or the bread wrappers. We had a lot of Abdullahs and Abrahams but no Mohammeds. I never met a Mohammed until I got to Miami many, many years later.

Niki had long, black hair that shined like silk and solid black eyes. I've heard such eyes called bedroom eyes. When you looked into her eyes you didn't want to stop looking. Maybe you were trying to find a light that wasn't really there, but anyhow?

She was the kind of a girl that could approach you as a stranger in the street, ask you a simple question and once you looked into her eyes, you would have completely forgotten what she asked. She was silly as hell. You just looked at her coming down the way and you started laughing.

Whenever we men talk of beautiful women with sex appeal we bring up Marilyn Monroe. Women can't seem to understand it. They say that Marilyn was just stupid and a tramp. Ah huh! Exactly! You have a problem with that?

I was into horoscopes in those days, and Niki had the same birthday as Marilyn Monroe. I think it was June 1. Everybody tries to analyze Marilyn's sex appeal. They give all kinds of sophisticated explanations. But the next time you see a film clip of Marilyn looking at a man, look at her eyes. She always has that look in her eye that most men only see in a woman's eyes on their wedding night.

Niki was movie star beautiful. She always had that look in her eye, and she was ever willing to be in bed with the man of her selection on any particular evening. The boys didn't call her loose, simply ever-willing and available for the right man. And the right man could change at any minute and all present were usually hoping that it was he.

The only man in the world who didn't want to sleep with Niki just happened to be one of our gang.

His name was Tommy. He dated Niki for a period and claimed that she was completely insane and that she had nearly gotten him killed on several different occasions. Most of the guys couldn't understand why something as insignificant as death would keep any young male off Niki's bones. What's the problem? When your number is up, your number is up. Everybody has got to go sometime. In any case, Tommy would have no part of Niki and for whatever this is worth guys, this seemed to make Tommy that much more irresistible to Niki. She wouldn't leave him alone.

Last year Niki showed up at the cottage looking for Tommy. She tried her best in her simple enticing way to seduce Tommy right in front of all of us. We were not opposed to watching. She kept asking Tommy to please go upstairs with her and make love. Tommy wouldn't do it. We were all on Niki's side of this debate. We all said; Please Tom, please. Finally after hours of teasing and coaxing, Tom turned to the rest of us and screamed.

"You guys actually think that it is fun to have sex with a raving lunatic?"

"Oh Tommy, look at her." Niki was just sitting there batting those long, black lashes of hers. "She's sorry."

"She's not sorry. She's F'in crazy."

"Oh that's not true. You're sorry, aren't you Niki?"

"I'm sorry Tommy. I didn't really think that my daddy would get that mad."

"Yah? With all them war pictures in his room, and that Japanese Samurai sword. He was going to cut the family jewels right off."

"A Samurai sword?"

"You should meet her father. He was on the Bataan Death March, for Christ sake. He's a maniac. He chased me for about five miles, and I was naked."

"Well, you weren't tossing your clothes over your shoulder as you ran, we can presume. I mean, you were in his bedroom having sex with his daughter."

"So?"

"Well, some fathers aren't accustomed to that. Right guys?"

"I wouldn't think so."

"No, I wouldn't imagine either," said Willie.

"Yah, well I don't care what the lunatic is used to. He ain't castrating me over his dimwit daughter."

"Okay, okay. But can't we just let bygones be bygones? Niki has said that she was sorry, right Niki?" we all negotiated.

"Hee hee hee."

"See, that means she's sorry, right boys?"

"Right, right. She looks sorry to me," we all agreed.

"Look, you guys want to have sex with this moron, go right ahead. I ain't touching her." We all turned and looked to Niki apprehensively. Suddenly she started to cry.

"Oh Tommy! Now look what you've done."

"I ain't done a thing."

"You've made her cry." We all felt very, very distraught for Niki. We all desperately wanted to comfort her – desperately, longingly, passionately.

"Okay, I'll tell you what," Tommy propositioned Niki. "I'll have sex with you upstairs, if first you have sex with each of these guys here."

"WHOOOOOaaaaa!" said us guys, jubilantly.

"I can't do that," Niki squeaked.

"Why the hell not?" demanded Tommy.

"Because."

"Because why?"

"Because you will just trick me. I'll do it with all of them first and then you won't do it with me."

"I will so."

"I don't believe you. You have sex with me first, and then I'll do it with them."

"Whoooaaaa!" (us guys, again)

"Okay let's go upstairs."

"No. First all of you go upstairs and take your clothes off," Niki pouted.

"Oh forget it. You're just playing games. The deal is off," Tom bellowed.

"NOOOOO!" A scream burst out from the peanut gallery. "We got no problem with that Tommy boy." Everybody ran for the bedroom upstairs and got undressed. We all lined up against the bedroom wall sweating passionately. Niki and Tommy came up into the bedroom. Niki couldn't stop giggling. She told Tommy to take off his clothes first. He stripped down without hesitation. Suddenly we all realized why Niki was so infatuated with Tommy. He was truly a "big" boy.

Niki just seemed to love the whole thing. She danced about the room slipping out of her things and grabbing and fondling Tommy at every chance she could work in. Moments later Tommy and she were busy on the bed and

57

we were all just watching and bursting at the seams. It seemed to take an eternity, but Tommy finally pulled himself away. He gathered up his clothes and as he left the room he said.

"Your turn."

We each looked down at Niki. She was on her back, leaning up on her elbows. She looked at each of us, and then in a voice like I had never heard before in my life, she yelled; "RAPE! HELP! HELP RAAAPPPEEE!" And she wouldn't stop. Most of us ran out of the room with our clothes in hand. Willie tried to stop her from screaming by putting his hand over her mouth.

That was not a good thing to do. She screamed bloody murder. We were all scrambling to get our clothes back on while Tom just stood there downstairs with a beer in his hand, shaking his head.

"I told you guys she was as nutty as a fruitcake, didn't I? She is out of her freakin mind."

"Let's get out of here - you too, Tommy boy. Leave her here by herself to talk to the cops."

We hopped into a vehicle and we were gone.

But that was last year. This year, we were older and wiser. When she came walking in the door, everybody stopped. We all said hello but cleared back from her by about six feet. She sat down in a chair at the foot of the stairs that led up to the bedroom. We weren't going to throw her out but we'd be very, very careful. Tom was out on the screened-in porch. He peeked in to see who had come in. When he saw Niki sitting there, he just threw his hands up and went back out onto the porch.

Niki giggled. We all roared. Willie was the first to speak. I don't remember what he said but Niki then responded by saying; "Oh, I remember you." Then she held up her index finger and thumb, indicating a tiny space between. Everybody roared again. If it didn't relate to sex,

Niki had no conversation whatsoever. She sat there for a few minutes giggling and smiling, but nothing was happening. Tommy wasn't interested, and we had all learned our lesson. Somebody went and got Niki a beer. Niki sat there, pulling her little dress up higher and higher, but even so, she seemed to be losing her audience. Then she asked.

"Is there anybody upstairs?"

"No."

"Could I use one of the bedrooms to freshen up?"

"Sure."

She proceeded up the stairs slowly and deliberately like a Las Vegas chorus girl or something. She was really crazy. We all just shook our heads. We now knew Tom's frustration. We would handle Niki with kid gloves, or a net.

She had been gone for quite awhile and we had momentarily forgotten about her. Suddenly somebody nodded to the stairway, and the room went quiet. The stairway was such that when a person came down the stairs, you would see their feet and then their legs and then their torso and last of all their face. Niki was proceeding down the stairway very slowly. By the time she got to where one could see her knees, it appeared as if she were naked ... once again.

She dropped another step and she was thigh deep. We were all viewing her from the far side of the room. No one was directly below the stairs. A few guys whistled and encouraged her to step down further. She made one more step and we could then see the edge of a towel that she had wrapped herself in. She took another step and she was now waist deep. The towel was very small. Little parts of flesh were trying to peek out here and there.

Niki then stretched out one leg and then another, slowly like a dancer or something. Well, really more like a stripper or something.

"Oh take off the towel Niki? What do you need a towel for?"

"Oh god, don't say that. Just leave her be. We don't want nothing like what happened last time."

"What? What happened last time?"

"Oh that's right, you weren't here. Just stay where you are. You can look but don't touch. And if she starts screaming rape, we're all outta here."

"OHHH."

"Come on Niki? Come on down? Let's see some cheek?"

Niki bent down and grinned at everybody though the banister dividers. She giggled.

"Not those cheeks Niki. You know what I mean."

She stood up once again, hiding her upper torso. She was only visible to slightly above the waist. She turned her side to the crowd and began to slide the seams of the towel apart revealing her whole leg and her thigh almost to her waist. She had everybody's attention. Then she turned to her backside, and slowly began to slide the towel up her butt to the screams and cat calls of all the boys. She had her butt totally exposed and was swaying it from side to side slowly when the front door was flung open.

It was Charlie standing there with his porkpie hat and a bag of groceries. Niki screamed and rushed back up the stairs. Charlie didn't know what was going on. We were all looking at the stairwell. He looked up curiously, and must have caught a peek of Niki giggling back up to her dressing room. We all stared at Chucky for a second. Nobody moved. What would Charlie do?

We certainly wouldn't hold it against him if he chose to leave, or to make some excuse and come back later. Nothing would ever be said about it one way or the other.

We might all have been on the downward step to perdition, but none of us were going to drag poor Charlie along. We all felt embarrassed for him. But not a one of us could wipe the stupid grins off our faces.

Charlie carried the groceries over to the table. Then grabbed a kitchen chair, pulled it over to the peanut gallery and leaned it up against the wall. Everybody roared and started clapping their hands. Charlie took out his pack of Lucky Strikes and started pounding them on his palm nervously as he always did.

"It's all clear Niki. It's just Charlie. Come on down."

Niki had a true sense for the dramatic. She sat down on one of the upper steps, and kicked one leg out in front of her. There was something about Charlie being there for Niki's strip show that made us all really, really happy. I don't know why. This certainly was no bachelor party. None of us knew what Charlie's experience was with women. Most of us were still in our teens. Charlie was twenty or twenty one. He wasn't exactly a big brother, but we respected him. Niki, as big a fruit-loop as she was, was really a once in a lifetime event. I have been alive a long time now, and I have seen none other quite like her. She was Marilyn Monroe in olive skin and sparkling black eyes. She gleamed. She just loved men. Don't ask me why. Niki knew how beautiful she was and she just wanted to show everybody or every man. She was a natural vaudeville queen.

We all kept teasing, whistling and coaxing until we had her returned to the naked thigh position. Every time she revealed a little more flesh we would all take a quick sneak peek at Charlie. When she turned her backside onto us once again and gave us that slow, naked, butt roll, Charlie threw his hands up to his head, and knocked his porkpie hat to the floor. Everybody clapped and whistled and slapped him on the back or the shoulder. He was really laughing. It was terrible. It was sinful. It was serious fun!

Niki was a joy. Little did she know the relief she was bringing on this particular occasion with all her foolishness. The constant hurting and torturous empathy was gone for a moment. We were just … alive. Charlie was alive. Some of us were laughing so hard that when we looked at Charlie we nearly cried.

And now Niki was downstairs. She was on the ground floor, the main stage. She was sashaying up and down. She was really into it. She would turn her back to us; spread open her towel like the wings of a butterfly; then peek coquettishly over the rim of the towel and bat her eyelashes.

"Oh Niki, Niki, we need a front shot. Come on, come on? We all love you. You're among friends."

That was Dutch. He was actually begging. We were all screaming with laughter. Tommy had come to the porch doorway and even he was laughing. But strangely enough Niki wasn't interested in Tommy at this moment. She was in the spotlight. It was hit the lights, tonight's the night, everything is coming up roses. It was so funny.

She then turned her front to the crowd as requested and spread her towel out once again - but in front of her, not behind her back. So now she was standing there naked but with the towel out in front of her so we could see nothing. She had to be rehearsing this stuff at home in front of a mirror or something. Everybody was laughing and slapping their thighs or whacking Charlie on the shoulder. Then she threw her towel up over her head and back around her body, but so fast that some of the guys missed it. The ones who got the quick shot roared but for many it had just happened too quickly.

"What? What did I miss?"

"You missed it all. Pay attention man! Pay attention."

What could she do now though? She had given us the back shot, the front shot, the whole deal. How was she going to top this? How was she going to exit without a riot?

She was really into the crowd. She saw how we were all huddling about Charlie. Suddenly, out of a clear blue sky, she ran over and jumped into his lap. The crowd hit the rafters and Niki knew that she was on the right track. You could see in her eyes that she was feeling everything out. She really didn't get it. Even for her, this was all an over reaction. But she knew something was going on.

She took off Charlie's hat and put it on her own head. Then grinned at everybody and waited for a reaction. She got it. She lifted her knees up to her chest and snuggled her head into Charlie's shoulder. Like a little kitten, she sat there purring. We all shifted our positions. With her knees up to her chest her butt is visible to certain portions of the crowd. She noticed where everyone was looking. She made a funny face and then pointed a finger and rubbed it for shame. The laughter grew louder.

She knew that she had something going on in Uncle Charlie's lap. She gave him a little peck on the cheek. Then she suddenly leaped out of Charlie's lap, grabbed her backside with one hand and looked down at Charlie's lap as if shocked and surprised. She put her hands onto her hips momentarily and then wagged a scolding finger into Charlie's face. Charlie's face went crimson. Niki's eyebrows rose, as she scanned the crowd, commenting favorably on Charlie's blushing. She then straddled Charlie's lap, and slowly swiggled herself down onto him. She nestled herself comfortably into Charlie's lap. Charlie's neck, forehead, cheeks and his whole face was red. No one could believe it. Niki then unwrapped her towel at her chest and wrapped it about Charlie's head as she nestled his face to her breasts. Willie had actually fallen to his knees and was slapping his palms to the floor. Dutch heard something and looked out the window.

"Anybody here expecting the cops?" he sputtered.

Niki jumped up off Charlie's lap and ran to the stairs.

"The cops ain't coming here Niki, don't stop." Willie pleaded.

Niki stopped running at the foot of the steps, looked down at Willie. He was on the floor on his knees and looked as though he was praying. She smiled. She then flipped off her towel, put her left arm up into the air as the towel, held in her other hand, draped down along her thigh. She posed there naked, looking like a Greek sculpture. Everyone groaned in unison and then applauded enthusiastically as she rushed up the stairs.

6   Overnight in the Big House

Instinctively, we all just knew that the coppers were not here for us. They must be looking for someplace else. Maybe one of them is a relative of Frank across the way. Frank was a retired cop from the Lowell area.

Dutch had gone from the window to the front door. He opened the door to greet the officers.

Just as he opened the door, like in some slap-stick movie, the first officer came in, tumbling like he was in the Olympics or something. He had obviously rushed up to our door and was in the attempt of putting his shoulder to it and knocking the thing down. We all looked down at the officer sprawled out on our kitchen floor. The officer, clearly combat ready with his billy club in one hand and his trusty handcuffs clipped onto his belt, was really a rather older dude. He had a big potbelly and a very, red face. He was fumbling all over the place trying to rise from the floor with some sort of athletic grace and dignity. He was not having much success.

Jack went over to try and help him up, but the old man had been watching too many Gang Busters episodes on the TV and he thought he was being attacked. He grabbed

Jack, pulled him to the mat and started welting him with his baton. Charlie at that moment had reached down towards the floor to pick up his porkpie hat, when a second officer lit into him. It was sheer panic when we saw that dumb flatfoot club Charlie across the skull with that stupid nightstick. Four of us were on top of his butt before you could say Jackie Robinson. We thought that we were doing pretty well until we saw a third officer escorting Charlie out the front door with Charlie's arm bent up behind his back.

"Hey man! You can't arrest Charlie."

That was me, and the next thing that I knew, we were both being stuffed into the back seat of a paddywagon. I didn't know what to think with Charlie and his red cells and his blue cells, or whatever. What would happen if they cut his head open and all the yellow cells came spilling out, leaving only the wrong cells left? Could he bleed to death, or what?

"Officer? Officer? Where are you taking my friends?"

"Here, get in and find out for yourself." Willie then came tumbling into the paddywagon. In another second or two Jack and Dutch were in there with us. In a matter of seconds we were off and heading downtown.

Downtown in Salisbury was just down the road. It took about thirty seconds to get to the police station. We were all immediately escorted to a cellblock, and each put into a separate cage. We were still yelling and screaming about the Constitution and the Bill of Rights and Women's Liberation and all the rest of it. The coppers just slammed the magic, metal "sprongers" on us and left us there to bitch to one another. As soon as they were gone, everybody's first question was;

"Hey, Charlie, you okay down there?" There was no answer for a moment or two. Then we heard somebody laughing.

"Who the hell thinks this is funny? Is that you Charlie?"

Charlie just kept laughing and laughing.

"Listen to that guy, will you? He thinks this is funny? Maybe we ought to see if we can get him a seat at the next state execution."

"Yah, or maybe we could get that flathead back in here and we could talk him into swatting Charlie on the head with his nightstick a few more times."

The more we joked the more Charlie laughed.

"Hey warden! We ain't going to eat this slop! Rattle, rattle, rattle. I wish I had a tin can that I could rattle on these iron bars."

"You know guys I hate to tell you this but this door don't open."

"No foolin'? Well if it ain't Albert Einstein."

"Hey, I'm not kidding."

"Hey Dutch. This is jail man. Don't you get it - J A L E, freakin jail. You're in the caboose, the big house, the Rock. We're here man."

"I know. I know. But what if this place catches on fire?"

"Whoa! You know, I never thought of that. Do you think that they would come and get us?"

"I've seen in the movies where the farmers come and rescue the horses who got locked in the barn."

"Yah, but horses are worth something. What the hell are you good for?"

"You know this is not the time to be bringing up stuff like this?"

"You're right."

"We could sue them."

"Yah, that would be good for your mother. She could retire and move to Florida."

Charlie was in hysterics.

"Hey Charlie, what do you think about all of this?"

"You guys are crazy; that's what I think."

"Hey? That's it. We'll plead insanity."

"Yah right, that should be 'no contest'."

"You know there are no pillows in here. How am I supposed to sleep?"

"There's no mattress in here either."

"Well, you know, that might be good news. They can't be planning on keeping us here for any length of time."

"We'll be out of here first thing in the morning. Don't you guys know anything?" Jack groaned.

"Ouuu, listen to him? It's mister professional jailbird over here. Okay Willie Sutton, give us the lowdown?"

"This is just the drunk tank. Come the morning, you cough up twenty-five bucks and you are free as a bird."

"Don't you have to be drunk to get into the drunk tank?"

"Noooo, you just have to be a loser and you passed."

"Thanks."

"You mean we don't get any breakfast or anything?"

"Yah right! How do you like your eggs over easy or what? What do you think this is a hotel or something?"

"What about my phone call? Don't I get to call somebody?"

"You know somebody?"

"No."

"So you saved a dime."

None of us slept all that well, but when morning came, Jack, the professional jailbird, had hit the nail right on the head. The day shift came strolling into the cellblock all smiles.

"Well, lookie, lookie here. We got a full house, Henry. Any of you deadbeats got any money?"

"Sure, we got plenty of money. My uncle is John D. Rocket-feller."

"Glad to hear it smartass. Anybody who's got twenty-five bucks, step up to your cell door."

68

We were all then escorted into the lobby.

"Don't we get a receipt?" Dutch whispered into my ear as he pushed up behind me.

"Don't worry about the receipt. Just worry about getting out that front door."

"I'm calling the N, double A, C P. They'll burn this place to the ground."

"You looked in the mirror recently? You're the wrong color, pal."

"Well who do I call?"

"I think you've gotta call the United Fund, or the Red Cross, or the International White Bread and Mayonnaise Association."

"They've got a White Bread Association?"

"Sure. They got something for everybody out there."

"What about the Salvation Army? I used to have an associate membership there?"

"You can try there. They'll be down here and trombone or tambourine these suckers to death."

"Serve them F'in right. Hey Warden, I ain't going to take this crap no more."

"Shhhhh, you butthead! These guys hear you and we'll be back in cellblock nine once again."

"Let 'em try it. I ain't scared of nuttin'. I could do another night in dare, standin' on my head."

"Hey? The Bowery Boys, right? What was that stupid guy's name with the baseball cap? You look like him."

"That was Mo."

"No no no. Don't give me no Mo of that."

"Ohhhhh. That was bad, man."

We were out into the street and we were all still laughing. We couldn't figure out what had really happened. We must have been getting pretty loud with the Niki floorshow. But, this was Salisbury Beach, summer party-town USA. This was the Fort Lauderdale of the

69

Northeast. We had police dogs and all the rest of it just two seasons ago over on the Hampton Casino. Everybody should be pretty much used to a little yelling and screaming.

We took a walk through the Center, and then stopped at Tony's for breakfast. In those days when you got ham and eggs, you got ham and eggs. You ordered bacon and you got a mound of it, with a pile of home fries and three eggs. You could even get a bowl of extra grease on the side to dip your toast into. Ahhh, for the good old days.

When we got back to the Cottage we were all too pooped to pop. I went upstairs to flop into my bed. I sat on the edge of my bed and began taking my shoes off when I heard a little peep. I looked over my shoulder, and there was Niki.

"You can't get into this bed."

"Why can't I?"

"Because I'm naked."

I lifted up the covers and sure enough, she was naked.

"Niki, I'm too tired for anymore of this. I'm going to sleep. You can do whatever you want." I flopped down on the top of the bed with my clothes still on and pulled a pillow up over my head.

I thought that I had been asleep for awhile when I opened my eyes, groggily. Niki was still there in the room. She was sitting in front of a large mirror. She was still nude, but was putting on her eye makeup. She looked into the mirror and saw me laying there with my eyes open.

"No peeking," she said.

I rolled over and faced the wall and in two seconds I was once again out like a light.

7   Charlie Gets Hungry for Lobster

The weekend was over and Charlie and I had the place to ourselves once again. The police had been driving by and checking us out just about every night. In fact, they kept checking on us for a few weeks after the Niki Naughty Night.

Charlie and I did our house cleaning chores; cleaned, washed this, that and the other thing, took a couple of loads of beer cans and bottles to the dump, and F B I-ed the neighborhood. Friday morning we took a ride. Charlie wanted to do a little sight-seeing. We ended up over in Marblehead.

Marblehead is a little New England coastal village. It is an old town with tiny, tiny streets. I mean streets that are even narrower than some of those back alleys in Boston. Most of these streets, of necessity, were one way. Many people rode bicycles all summer around there. It is a "quaint" New England village.

Charlie just loved lobster. New England lobster was his number one favorite food. Whenever we went to Bishop's or any fancy restaurant, Charlie would order lobster. Sometimes he would order two. Well, as we were plowing around Marblehead, we ended up at this dockside area. There were a couple of boats unloading their catch. Charlie hopped out of the car and went prancing over. Charlie was sort of bullish. He walked with his head down and shoulders forward, and every time that he exited the car he was lighting up a cigarette. He started talking to this guy on a boat who looked like he should have his picture on a can of tuna fish.

"You sell any of these Lobsters?"

"Yup, I sure do."

"What you get for 'em?"

"Well ... depends."

"Depends on what?"

"First depends on how many you want to buy."

"How many do you think we ought to get, Rich?"

"I can never eat more than three or four myself."

"How about thirty?"

"Thirty lobsters?" I exclaimed.

"Forty?"

"Forty?" I couldn't believe Charlie was serious.

"Okay, how much would fifty lobsters cost us?" Charlie asked the man.

"Well, I would have to get at least seventy-five cents apiece, if'n you bought fifty of 'em."

"Seventy-five cents each?" I spit in disbelief.

"Well, I'm going to tell you sonny, you go right into that building over there and you'll pay double that for the same darn lobsters. Once I get them off this boat and drag them across the way over there, the price doubles - sometimes even more than doubles."

"Seventy-five cents is good enough," Charlie said. "Count us out fifty of them."

The man started counting them off into a box lined with seaweed. In the middle, every now and then, he would get to talking and forget where he was at. Charlie would say, "You were at twenty-five."

"Well, let's just say twenty three so nobody gets cheated. Don't want nobody to say old Captain Mohab cheated some city slickers, do we?"

"No, we sure don't." Charlie looked at me and winked.

I don't know how many lobsters we actually got for thirty-seven-fifty, but we had a trunk full.

From Marblehead we went to Ipswich. Charlie said lobsters just ain't right without a bucket of steamers. So, we picked up a few gallons of Ipswich steaming clams, a big tub of real butter, and then a couple of bags of sweet corn and some onions at a roadside stand. We were going to do it to it this weekend. Charlie was hungry for a New England Clambake and we were going to have one.

On the way back to the cottage Charlie stopped at St. Ann's in Salisbury. Friday was confession day, if you remember. I decided to stop in and see what St. Ann's looked like. As we approached the door, I said; "Well, can't say you ain't got nothing to tell the good Father this week, Charlie boy." Charlie laughed.

It was a nice church, a real nice church. Catholic churches really never look chintzy. This one didn't have marble communion rails like St. Mary's did back home in Lawrence. But it had some nice looking wood stuff.

Charlie went and got in line over at one of the stalls. I sat back and watched for girls who came into church with somebody else and didn't go to confession themselves. I had a buddy who went to church on Sundays primarily to scope out any girls who didn't go to communion. This was a good sign for a bad boy. If a girl was already in the state of sin and couldn't go to communion on Sunday, what the heck did she have to lose? This was creative thinking I thought at the time. Not going to confession when you're right there in the church, I felt had to be in the same category. When he originally told me his communion strategy, I laughed, but then every Sunday thereafter I did the same thing.

A very attractive blond girl came in with a couple of friends. They sat down in front of me. The blond girl's two friends went to confession. The pretty blond didn't go. She just stayed there in the pew kneeling and praying. I felt an immediate attraction towards her. When they had all finished saying their penance and got up to leave, I nodded to the blond, smiled and said hello. She looked down at me sitting there with my arms draped over the back of my bench and sporting my best Jack Nicholson grin and said;

"I went earlier today."

"Right. Did I say anything?"

"No, but I don't have to be clairvoyant to read a mind like yours."

"Well, ahh … thank-you very much. People have always said that I was open minded."

"Yah!"

Well, everybody was more than happy to pitch in for the clambake. We borrowed a bunch of pots and pans and started cooking everything that afternoon. Charlie had even picked up a bunch of nutcrackers and some bibs with a picture of a lobster on them.

First we all drank a shot of the broth from one of the buckets containing the corn, onions, steamers and lobsters. You drop a little butter into it and sprinkle some pepper on top and wow!

We all ate lobsters, clams and corn on the cob until we could eat no more, and we still had pots full of everything. Fifty something lobsters was a little heavy.

"What are we going to do with all this stuff?"

At just that moment a group of young ladies in their beach attire came strolling by on their way back from getting wet and sandy. We had seen them a few times in the recent past. They were staying in a cottage at the end of our road. Tommy recognized one of the girls. Her name was Helen. She was another Syrian girl and her daddy owned a diner up on Lawrence Street across from Hadenscofield. We called it Haden's sco-field. There's a lot of funny things like that. I think that I was sixteen before I ever realized that my "birfday" related to the day that I was born or that "prencils" were really pretzels and vengetables were vegetables and badaydoes were potatoes. Then we had ... and blessed is the fruit of thy wound Jesus ... I prege allegiance to the flag ... one nation, invisible with truth and justice for all.

"Hey girls!" Charlie beamed, bulling out onto the stoop. "Anybody feel like eating a couple of lobsters?"

"You're kidding?"

Charlie scuffled back inside and returned to the doorway brandishing a fine and mellow crimson crustacean. He waved it above his head as he stood in the doorway. The girls just stood there for a moment staring at one another. Then a couple of them shrugged their shoulders and the next thing we knew we had a cottage full of girls with lobster bibs on, munching down on our fine fare.

Chucky was a good host. He kept heating up butter and slopping down platters full of corn on the cob. All the guys were flirting with somebody. The girls didn't seem to mind at all. This might be a good technique? But could we afford to do this every weekend? We would just take one weekend at a time.

The girls ended up hanging out for the evening. We never stopped eating. We all drank some beer. We played some records and danced. We had a good old time. In the middle of the festivities Tommy elbowed me and nodded his head over to Charlie. Charlie was in the kitchen with

Helen. He was leaning up against the sink with his porkpie hat jauntily askew and Helen was staring up into his eyes, dreamily, as they basked in the light of pre-adult small talk.

"Ought oh," I said with a laugh, "more material for Father Kelly next Friday." Tommy sputtered and then went back to business.

The girls were all hometown girls from somewhere in the area. Willie found a girl from Lowell. Helen was as I said from Lawrence. Dutch met a girl from Andover. There was another girl from Methuen. All in all it was a perfect day - wine, women, song and fine food. A great day, indeed!

8   Helen

Helen was a "nice" girl. She was no Niki, but pretty …
in an average way. She wasn't the kind of girl that anyone
went running after. She was, more or less, the kind that
most boys marry. She was sweet as could be.

As far as we could tell, Charlie wasn't really
encouraging her. She just seemed to show up every now
and then. When she did, she always gravitated towards
Charlie. After a bit, every time we saw her coming down
the road we would tease Charlie.

"Here comes your girlfriend, Charlie."

Charlie wasn't encouraging her, but he wasn't chasing
her away either. He was attracted to her, and that was
obvious, but he didn't seem to be eager to be moving this
relationship forward.

One quiet night she came strolling by alone. We called
her in. There were two of us plus Charlie. We all talked
and had a couple of beers. It started to get late and the
conversation was winding down. Tommy put a Frank
Sinatra record on and asked Helen for a dance. She
accepted. So then I asked her to dance with me on the next
song. And for at least an hour or so Tommy and I were
waltzing around with Helen. Charlie just sat there puffing
on a Lucky and sipping on a little ugly Kruger bottle.

Finally Helen went over, bashfully, and stood in front of Charlie with her arms stretched out. Charlie stared at her for a moment, then snuffed out his cigarette and got up and danced.

The three of us kept taking turns after that. After a bit, Helen was really subdued. With each additional dance she just fell softer and softer into our arms as we sloughed about the place. Her eyes were getting droopy and dreamy. I would suppose she never had such continuous attention before in her life. She was finally so rag-doll like that I felt that if I took my arm from around her waist she would just slide down to the floor and swoon into a dreamy sleep. Charlie picked her up next. I went to the fridge and got out two beers. I brought one over to Tom, handed it to him, and nodded towards the door. With Charlie's back to us, and Helen's eyes closed and her head pressed into his shoulder, we slipped out the door.

Tommy and I went down to the 5 O'clock Club. We really didn't have much to say to one another. But finally Tommy says:

"Well, what do you think?"

"About what?"

"About Helen and Chuck?"

"I don't know."

"Do you think they will get it together tonight?"

"I certainly hope so."

"Do you really?"

"Don't you?"

"I don't know."

"What don't you know?"

"I don't know if it is the right thing to do."

"What do you mean the 'right' thing?"

"Well, do you think that Helen knows about Chucky?"

"I don't know."

"Don't you think that it is important?"

"I don't know."

"Wouldn't you want to know?"

"I already know."

"I know you know. Jesus Christ! Wouldn't you want to know if you were her?"

"I suppose."

"Damn right, you suppose!"

"But, I ain't really thinking about her. Don't you think that she will get over it?"

"Oh yah, sure. She'll get over it. It might take twenty or thirty years. You know, maybe by the time Chucky junior is in the Marine Corps or something."

"Chucky junior? Come on!"

"What? A little poke here and a little poke there and that's what happens."

"Well, you've got to be careful?"

"Sure, be careful? Your mother was trying to be careful, and look what the hell happened."

"Hey, you trying to tell me that I wasn't a "love" child?"

"Yah, you were a love child all right. Me too. The whole F'in neighborhood. We are all love childs. All three hundred and fifty million of us."

"Gee Tommy. You're making me feel bad. I mean if my own mother didn't really want me?"

"Yah. Deal with it. You'll get over it, too. The more I think about it, I really don't think that Chucky should be messing with anybody."

"How about Niki?"

"Niki? Now Niki would be O.K. You don't have to worry about her remembering anything. She don't have any mind. She couldn't remember anything even if she wanted to."

"How come when it comes to Niki you ain't worried about any little Chucky junior?"

"Whoa, that is a scary thought. Do you think that Niki could really have a baby?"

"You don't think that she could?"

"Niki? Niki with a baby? Wow! Niki at a PTA meeting? Niki changing diapers and doing the laundry? I don't think so."

"You're funny, you know that? All that time that you were fooling around with Niki and you never thought of a little Tommy junior?"

"Me and Niki, you mean?"

"Exactly! A little poke here, a little poke there and mama, mama, where's my papa?"

"No, no, no. That ain't going to happen to me. I know how to pull out."

"Yah, so did your father."

"Okay, okay! Good luck to Chucky. Let him have his fun. What do I care."

By the time we got back to the cottage Helen and Chucky were gone.

As the days and weeks went by, Chucky and Helen became an "item" ... "a thing." Whatever, they became buddies, friends. Every weekend Helen would stop by and shortly thereafter they would disappear. They went to the beach by themselves sometimes. A couple of times she came by with a picnic basket. They went bowling a few times, Chucky had mentioned. They went to an occasional movie, and any number of evenings and afternoons just hanging out with the gang at the cottage. There were no outward displays of emotion. A little holding hands, an arm draped over Helen's shoulder, a smile, a little peck on the cheek to say goodbye. No big deal.

One Friday I was over to St. Ann's with Charlie. Helen and some of her friends just happened to be there going to confession also. I said hi as she passed by me sitting in the back of the church. She said hello, looked at me curiously and went along. A second or two later she was back beside my pew staring at me. I looked up at her.

"Why are you looking at me like that?" she asked.

"Like what?"

"You know like what."

"No I don't know, like what. I haven't the slightest idea."

"You were looking at me funny."

"Listen, with a face like this, a lot of people think I'm looking at them funny."

"You weren't thinking anything?"

"I might have been. I've been known to do that sometimes."

"What were you thinking?"

"I was thinking - whatever happened to Norman Mailer?"

"Who's he?"

"I really don't know. Maybe that's why I was wondering about him?"

She gave me a peculiar look, then left.

She was right, I had been thinking. I was wondering how far their relationship had progressed. I had flashes of them in bed together or making love on a moonlit night down on the beach. I was thinking of what Chucky junior might look like. I thought that she might be there tonight confessing her sins. And if this was all true, what would Charlie be confessing to? If the priest knew all of Charlie's situation, what would he be telling Charlie to do? Say three Our Fathers and three Hail Marys? What business was it of mine, anyway? Was Helen picturing little picket fences and a small house up on the hill? If this was all true, what was Charlie thinking? This really wouldn't be good, would it? Then again, what was I thinking? There was no indication that Chucky was having sex with Helen. And so what if he was? But if so, shouldn't somebody be telling Helen about Charlie's future? Yes, somebody should be telling Helen, but it shouldn't be me. Not me man. This was all none of my business. I ain't God. I ain't even Father Kelly.

The summer was passing by rapidly. Wouldn't be long and it would be September and we would all be down here partying by ourselves.

This was another party night at our place. Niki was there doing one of her comedy routines. Helen was there with Chucky in the kitchen. Four or five of us were playing Forty-fives at the kitchen table. There was music playing and a lot of laughing and joking going on.

Charlie had been acting funny all week. Helen was as close up to him in public as I had yet seen. He turned his head towards her and she kissed him. He didn't respond very well. I looked at him. He looked away. Then he took Helen by the hand and went out onto the back porch. Everybody had been acting as if they hadn't seen anything. But nobody missed that kiss on the part of Helen - and Chucky's face? Not good. Not angry or annoyed, but not happy. All of us at the card table looked at one another. Jack raised his eyebrows. Tommy shook his head negatively. The time had come. No doubt about it.

It seemed like a very long moment that they were on the back porch. There were a lot of stupid mistakes being made at the card table. Forty-fives was a game of strategy like Bridge or something, and everybody's strategy was suddenly out on the back porch.

The back porch door swung open with a burst. Helen rushed through the room. She put her hands up to her face and began weeping. She was heading for the front door. Dutch opened it for her and she rushed out into the street. She stopped for a second in the middle of the road. Then she started running towards her cottage. The feelings were so thick in the room that my glasses fogged. I started to tear-up slightly. Chucky appeared at the backdoor and I stopped instantly.

"Okay. You got any sevens?" Jack said to me.

"No, go fish," I said.

Everybody looked at us as if we were crazy. But Jack was right. This game of Forty-fives was over. Nobody was paying any attention. Nobody was making the right plays.

Chuck's eyes were all red and his cheeks were moist. He leaned back against the stove. He took out a handkerchief and blew his nose. The room was extremely quiet. Nobody knew what to do. Do we all get up and leave Charlie to himself? Do we act as if nothing happened and ask Charlie if he wants to play cards? Do we ...

"Can I ask you guys a question?" Charlie said.

The place went very quiet.

"Sure ... shoot," Willie said.

"Do you guys know about me? ... About my condition?"

We all hung our heads. I heard a voice. I didn't know whose it really was. I think it was Willie again.

"Yah, we know, Chucky."

"I mean ... do you know the whole story? I know you all know that I'm sick but do you know ... do you know that I'm going to die?"

Phewwww. It was getting tough to breathe. I got up and opened the back door. I began to fan the door, back and forth, trying to create a breeze. I couldn't look at Charlie.

"We know, Chucky," Jack said.

Charlie pursed his lips and started bobbing his head up and down, knowledgeably. He took out his handkerchief and wiped his eyes. With his face hidden under his handkerchief he wept in a low, cracking tone.

"You guys are good. I really couldn't tell. Sometimes ..." he sniffled and blew his nose again, "sometimes I thought for sure that you guys had to know ... and then sometimes I just couldn't really tell." We all had the sniffles now.

There was a very long pause. None of us had anything to say. Finally Charlie said, "Thanks."

We were all pretty shocked. "Thanks?" somebody wondered out loud. "Thanks for what?"

"Thanks for treating me ... like a normal person." Charlie started to cry.

Everybody started to cry.

"Well, damn," Jack finally sputtered, reaching into his back pocket for his own handkerchief. "You SHOULD be thanking us. It wasn't easy treating you like a "normal" person. To tell you the truth it has not been easy all these years to treat any of these guys like normal people. I've had a bitch of a time faking the whole thing."

We all started laughing and crying at the same time. Willie jumped up and went over and hugged Charlie and bawled onto his shoulder.

"Okay, let's not start getting romantic here," Charlie croaked.

Everyone then took a turn. Some just shook Charlie's hand and patted him on a shoulder, others hugged. A couple of guys kissed him on the cheek or the forehead. I was still fanning the door and bawling my eyes out. Finally when everybody was done, Charlie peeked over at me with his teary eyes. I looked and couldn't stop crying, but for a second I choked everything up, I threw my hands at him and coughed between bursts of sobbing ... "Oh screw you. I'll send you a card." Between the tears, everybody roared again.

"I'd like to see them cops raid this place now," Willie said. "A whole room full of grown men, crying and hugging and kissing one another."

Jack looked around the room, dubiously. "A whole room full of grown men? I'm confused, and I sure as hell ain't about to kiss you yet!"

"Oh yah," Charlie said getting some control. "I want to thank you guys for that too. That was the best night of my whole life. I had never been in a jail cell before."

"Well, Charlie," Jack mumbled, "we could arrange that again right now."

"No no, thanks a bunch, but once was enough. This has really been a great summer - the best summer of my life."

At that point somebody said, "Do any of you guys remember the time ..." and then the talk of the Good Old Days began. Reminiscing about our "childhood days" on the Corner was one laugh after another. Then it got sloppy again. Somebody remembered some mistreatment that they personally had dumped onto Charlie. Then one by one everybody began to confess and ask for Chucky's forgiveness. I had one of my own.

One night coming home from a Central Catholic basketball game we all had gotten into a snowball fight. I had finally picked up a huge hunk of combination snow and ice. Charlie was on the other side of the street. I never, in my wildest dreams, thought that I could reach him with it. I gave it my best shot-put effort, and it soared. When I realized that it was going to make it to its intended destination, Charlie's head, I screamed; "Duck Charlie! Duck!" Needless to say, Charlie didn't duck and it smacked him good. It hit him so hard it put him down to his knees. I ran across the street. I thought that I had killed him. He finally got up off his knees, but he was crying. We "tough guys" never cried. None of us ever cried as kids. When I saw those tears, I knew that I had really hurt him. I said things like; "Okay Charlie, just punch me in the mouth. Come on. I owe you one. I don't care. Hit me as hard as you can." But he wouldn't do it.

So during this confession period I said. "You remember the time I hit you with that pile of snow, Charlie?" Ouuu!! Charlie's face got all serious. He remembered all right.

"That was no chunk of snow. That was an iceberg."

"Noooo?" I pleaded. "It wasn't an iceberg. It had a little ice mixed in with it maybe, but it wasn't an iceberg."

"It was a block of ice. A huge block of ice," Charlie told everybody. "I really thought that he had knocked my head off with it. It put me to my knees." Everybody in the room looked at me. I shrugged apologetically. "I thought I was a dead man. I saw stars. Everything blanked out." Charlie went on. Nobody was laughing anymore. Everybody was looking at me. I wanted to crawl into a hole.

"Oh come on Charlie? You know I didn't mean it?"

"Yah, you didn't mean it. Sure."

"Well, what about the time" ... and finally we were onto another adventure - somebody else's adventure.

We all sat up most of that night shooting the bull with Charlie and belching up the old times. We drank a lot of beer too.

None of us asked about Helen. It was really none of our business. Truthfully most of the guys never talked about their personal romances or female relationships.

Next weekend it was just business as usual, until Helen appeared at the front door. It got quiet for a second, but then we all went right into our "normal" routine.

"Hi Helen. How are you?" a few of the guys ventured.

Charlie began pacing back and forth in the kitchen. Helen went back to speak with him. It was once again awkward time. Everybody sitting at the kitchen table moved elsewhere until finally Helen and Chucky were pretty much alone in the kitchen. It was such a small place though, privacy was at a minimum.

We all began talking louder trying to drown out their conversation. Helen cornered Charlie in front of the stove. She was talking softly and trying to touch him and move close to kiss him. He was having none of it. Right or wrong, it was clear; Charlie had come to a decision about this situation. He had been in and out of the hospital for the last couple of weeks and maybe that had something to do with it. Nobody really knew.

We knew that he was going to die, and we were told that it could happen at anytime. We knew that fact from the very beginning. It seems a little strange to me now, that nobody ever questioned the doctor's verdict, not even Charlie. The doctors said that Charlie was going to die, and that was it. Charlie would die. No questions asked. Even with Charlie, there was no; "I'm going to fight this. I'm going to beat this thing." I can't remember one person ever questioning the prognosis. The doctors said that someone was going to die and the only question was - when? Seems peculiar today.

Suddenly Helen stamped her foot onto the floor and shouted; "That's my business! You should let me worry about that." Charlie took her by the hand and they went outside onto the back porch once again.

This was an interesting time in the lives of a bunch of basic regular guys. A bunch of guys, who never seemed to think a heck of a lot about anything, were now all sitting in their chairs deep in meditation. Some just staring at a wall; others peeling the labels off their beer bottles; some lighting up their cigarettes. Each one concerned with thoughts that had never entered their minds before; trying to make decisions on things that were never before even in existence. Charlie was a dead man. Do dead men have any rights? Can a dead man have a girl friend? Yes, Charlie was a dead man, all right, but he was still breathing. Can't he hug somebody? Can't he fall in love? He's not Jesus Christ. He's not here to account for the sins of mankind. Can't he have sex with a grown girl if she wants to be with him? He's just Charlie. Charlie with the porkpie hat. Charlie who smoked too much. Charlie with the penny loafers and the snapping leather heels. Charlie nobody. Charlie the street kid from the "gang" on the Corner.

We were all like some kind of a judge and jury, weren't we? Sitting back in our never ending lives making judgments on how another man should die or live his life - what he should do; how he should act. But maybe that wasn't all of it. Weren't we all in the same boat? Charlie was just first in line? Were we not just children watching and trying to figure a guide for our future behavior? Were we not forming principles? Were we not looking for standards, maybe? Were we not just human beings ourselves, doing what it is that human beings do? Figuring it all out?

What's it all about Alfie?

The backdoor opened and Charlie returned to the kitchen, alone. Almost simultaneously the conversation burst open once again, as if all of our tongues were attached to a string that was connected to the doorknob. Charlie didn't notice any of us. He took out a pack of Luckies from his pocket and began pounding it on his palm as he always did before opening a new pack.

This had to be heavy for Charlie. This was a heavy thing for a twenty year old. He was so brave. This whole situation was so tragic and he was so brave. He was a good example. We never heard one sputter of regret out of him. No, "Why me?" No, "What did I do to deserve this?" No pouting, no sulking, no crying - really no self-pity crying. Okay, enough of this ... next Chapter.

9   The Hospital

Charlie was spending more and more weekdays at the hospital, but he wasn't missing any weekends at the beach. We had a big hamburger and "yes 'em, it's Essem" hot dog extravaganza on the beach one weekend. We bought a bunch of T-bone steaks on another weekend. Charlie loved to do the grilling. The visits to the hospital were getting so frequent that we all decided to make it a point to drop by whenever he was in. One never knew. It could happen any day. We all were very, very intent in getting in our last good-byes. We certainly didn't want to hear the news that Charlie had died, over the telephone, or read about it in the newspaper.

Whenever we walked into Charlie's hospital room the faces on his mother and father or any guests would just beam. If everybody gets five or fifteen minutes of fame, as they claim, we were getting ours. We were celebrities. Anybody who was in the room when we walked in, would leap out of their chairs and run for the door. We would say to his mom and dad; "You don't have to leave. You guys can stay right here and visit."

"Oh no no no no no ... You guys are Charlie's friends. You have a lot to talk about. We can be here anytime."

If there was a nurse in there, even her face would beam. We would all look at one another wondering the same thing; "You know that nurse? Why is she looking at us like that?" Oftentimes a nurse would try to guess who was who.

"Let me see," she would say pointing to one of us. "You are Dutch and you are Tommy ... and you are ... ahh?"

What was this all about? Obviously Charlie was talking about us. Everybody, excluding his mom and dad, knew about our night in the "Big House." Everybody wanted to meet Niki. It was a laugh. It made us all feel pretty good. We really didn't think that Charlie was having all that great a time. We certainly weren't, but he certainly was. Charlie was like our cottage tomcat. He just strolled around the cottage and rubbed on this one and that one. Every now and then somebody reached out and gave a little stroke. Nothing big was going on here, but Charlie must have loved it. He was just telling everybody about his summer adventures. It made us all feel great, and we started acting somewhat like stand-up comedians every time we walked in. We really didn't have to do much. We would say; "Hey, how you doin'?" and everybody would spit-up with laughter. It would have been interesting to hear what Charlie had been telling them about us. That certainly had to have been some good stuff.

When Charlie was out and about, he would pop into the Y and we'd head for the beach or buzz about town. This was a crazy disease because he never seemed sick. He was always the same - just sometimes he would be lying in a hospital bed, or sometimes he would be driving an automobile.

As we were scooting about Lawrence one time, we went by what I thought might have been Helen's father's diner.

"I think that's Helen's dad's joint," I said matter-of-factly.

90

"You think so?"

"Yah."

"Let's go get a cup of coffee."

"Don't matter to me."

We parked the buzzmobile out in front and went bulling into the diner. The bar or counter, with all of the little swivel stools with the red seats, was to the right and the tables and booths were to the left. We chose the counter and a stool. A guy waited on us. He was probably Helen's father. He looked typical for a diner owner - like half truck driver, half gangster. Charlie's cup of coffee turned into ham and eggs, home fries and pancakes. I got some scrambled eggs, baked beans and toast. Helen came out of the kitchen with our plates. When she saw us, she stopped her father, whispered into his ear, and gave the plates to him. She then returned to the kitchen. Charlie saw her. He just grinned to himself. The father brought our stuff over, and was very friendly. He came around the counter and sat at a stool next to Charlie.

"I feel like I know you," he said patting Charlie on the back very gently and with obvious extreme care; like he was afraid that he might break something. Then he just sat there leaning on the counter and staring at Charlie.

"Good eggs," Charlie told him.

"Yah . . . ahh . . . yah - they're good eggs. So, how you feeling anyway?"

"Oh, feeling good - great. How you feeling?" The man smiled. "You're lucky to have a daughter like Helen. She is a really fine girl."

"She is. She really is. She's a great kid." Then he just sat there staring at Charlie and not saying anything. After what seemed like forever, he patted Charlie on the back again and as he got up from his stool said. "Enjoy your breakfast."

"I sure will," Charlie said with a big smile putting down his knife and fork, and sticking out his hand. The man shook Charlie's hand, and nodded his head up and down. Then he went back behind the counter and into the kitchen.

We finished our breakfast, but no Helen. She didn't come out of the kitchen. I don't know what I expected her to do.

Charlie got another cup of coffee and just sat there staring at the wall. I don't really know what I expected Charlie to do either. It kind of felt like ... goodbye. Like he was trying to say goodbye, but he didn't know how to do it. Helen wasn't going to say anything and Charlie had burned all the bridges and sunk all the boats. He rubbed on his chin as he sat there. I thought that maybe he was going to get up and head back into the kitchen but ...

"Let's get out of here!" he said.

We went up to the cashier by the front door, paid our check and stepped out onto the sidewalk. We stood out there on the sidewalk staring around at the old tenement houses for a moment or two. I wasn't moving, if he wasn't moving. It really felt kind of cold to be just driving away, but Chucky headed for the car.

We were both inside the car when Helen came running out the door. I nudged Charlie and he got out and went over to meet her. She just stood there with her head down and her arms at her sides. She was crying, of course. I rolled up the window. I didn't really want to hear any of this. She put both hands up and covered her face. He put his arms around her and pulled her to him. They just stood there. Her covered face buried into his chest and his arms holding on tight - no words.

Finally he leaned his head back and pushed her head up by placing a finger under her chin. He gave her a little kiss. She looked up at him. Then threw her arms around his neck and kissed him long and lovingly. When the kiss ended, she pulled away without a glance and ran back inside the diner.

As we were about to pull off, I saw her standing by the cafe' window. Her head was just visible above the row of checkered curtains. What a face on her. I couldn't let Charlie go without seeing this. I poked him and thumbed his view towards the window. He leaned toward me and peeked up through my window. Helen saw him and tried her best to smile. Chucky looked at her, then gave her the old Navy double thumbs up. She put up her thumbs, hesitantly, over the curtain. Charlie straightened up behind the wheel, started the car and as we pulled out he leaned on the horn a few times and we were gone.

Well, there we were in the hospital once again. We we're about to go into Charlie's room and a nurse came out the door. She was crying. She looked up at us, then brightened up.

"He's going to be glad to see you guys," and she smiled broadly.

That was good news. We all looked at one another. Each of us had the same idea when we had seen that nurse's face. He was dead. But he certainly couldn't be glad to see us, if he was dead.

"Great!" we said, figuring that she must have been crying routinely, or just for the hell of it. Dutch put his hand to the doorknob, and then she said putting her hand onto my sleeve;

"If you have any good-byes to say, you had better do them now."

"Shit! Shit! Shit! Shit!"

We didn't hesitate for a second. We pulled a Charlie and bulled our way right into the room with our "thanks for treating me normal" facades and beaming smiles.

Charlie's mother and father nearly knocked us over on their way out of the room. We were there to do our job. Suck it up; light the lights - tonight's the night; everything coming up roses.

Charlie didn't look any different than he ever did. He was sitting up in the bed smoking a cigarette.

Tommy said; "Don't you know them things will kill you?"

Chucky did a double take and then just stared at Tommy, cynically amused.

"Yah ... right," Tommy said. "Got ya."

We all just half smiled and shook our heads dubiously.

Dutch started right in with a tale about his traumatic experience at the grocery store that day. It was good for about thirty seconds and then started to peter out.

I told Charlie that I had been to Helen's diner for breakfast that morning. He perked up.

"How is she?"

"She's good. She really looks good. She got herself a cat."

"A cat?"

"Yah. She says that she got it because it was the colors of your porkpie hat."

"Wow! Must be an ugly cat."

"She named it Charlie."

"Let me take that back. It must be a great looking cat."

Everybody took a turn at the small talk, but Charlie kept drifting. You could tell. We would be talking and he would be just staring out the window into the darkness. Pretty soon we were simply talking to one another and Charlie wasn't paying any attention at all. Then Willie said; "Listen to us. Here we are standing here jibber jabbering all our bullshit while poor Charlie's laying here dying."

.

94

"Oh no! Don't ever think like that. I love the bullshit. You guys have the best bullshit around. I don't know what I would have done without it."

"So what's the story Chucky? They tell us tonight that things don't look too good?"

"Well, I don't know. It's that red cell, white cell stuff again. One of them keeps eating the other one and it seems to be getting out of control."

"So?"

"So, your body can only live with a certain balance of these things."

"What about the medicine?"

"It only works for so long."

"And this is about as long as it is going to go?"

"I guess. That's what they tell me." We all just stood there around the bed - heads down; thinking the same thing - ain't this a bitch. "You know it is kind of funny, I know that I am supposed to be dying. Everybody keeps telling me that I'm dying. But I'll be damned if I can. Sometimes, I would just like to get it over with. But, I don't know how. I just don't know how to do it."

"Yah. That's one thing that everybody has to learn on their own, don't they?"

"Seems that way."

We all kind of huddled around one side of the bed, every now and then reaching out and touching Chucky on the leg or the arm to remind him about something that had happened in the past. We went through as many of the old routines as we could possibly remember. None of us wanted to leave, but we had to. It was crunch time, and this was the time for family.

One by one we said our good-byes and went over to the bed and gave Charlie a hug or shook his hand. Most of us just said goodbye. Dutchy said; "See you tomorrow." Charlie perked up, smiled, nodded his head and winked. I was the last one at the hospital room door. I was just about to go out when I stopped and closed the door in front of me.

"Charlie? One last thing?"

"Yah Richie?"

"I really didn't mean to hit you with that damn block of ice."

"See! See, you finally admitted it. It WAS a block of ice."

"I know it was. I know it was, damn it, but I never thought that I could throw it that far. I really didn't"

"Yah sure," Charlie said with a grin.

"Charlie?" I started to cry. "I'm serious. You have got to say that you forgive me for that or I'll never get it out of my mind."

Charlie grabbed his cigarettes and lit one up. He sat there for a moment blowing smoke up into the light fixture."

"Richie," he said. "I know that you didn't mean it. You would never intentionally try to hurt a darn thing in your whole life. You just ain't got it in you."

I sighed. I felt like a big weight had been lifted off my shoulders.

"Good luck Chucky. We all love ya, buddy."

"I know you do. You guys were the best thing that ever happened to me. I'll never forget what you all did or my last summer at Salisbury Beach."

I couldn't speak. I waved goodbye and then I left the room.

We all just leaned up against the wall outside the room for awhile. Charlie's mom and dad came over and they shook all of our hands. Then they went back into the hospital room.

They were not doing good. Their faces looked like they had been crying constantly for six months. They each took a deep breath, sucked it all up, and tried to conjure up their "it's a wonderful life, Jimmy Stewart faces." They opened the door and entered Dante's abyss.

"We really ought to get out of here," Willie suggested. "This is family time."

"Right."

"You know, I'm never going to forget what Charlie said."

"What?"

"About not knowing how to die. 'I know that I am supposed to die. I just don't know how to do it,' he said. Ain't that something! He don't know how to die?"

"Me neither."

10   The Wake

During that evening, some time around two in the morning, Charlie's white blood cells lost the battle to the red blood cells or vice versa. He died. It seemed impossible. There he was sitting up in his hospital bed puffing on a Lucky and a few hours later, on his way to being embalmed.

That weekend there would be no party or cookout at Salisbury Beach. We would all be going to a wake and funeral.

My cat, Blackie; my dog, Rex; my Uncle Joe; my dad; and my buddy, Chucky - at least with Charlie we had plenty of time for good-byes, and hellos, for conversations, and companionship, even confessions and absolutions. My dad was quietly sitting at the dinner table one night, and he was dead the next morning. No hellos or good-byes, no nothing.

For some reason I can't remember which funeral home waked Charlie. It should have been Rosinski's. They were the Polacks, and Charlie was a Polack. My father was at Rosinski's. My father was Irish. So much for that logic. I think Charlie was at Breen's. I remember the inside of the room clearly. It wasn't Rosinski's.

The gang from the Corner had the first row directly in front of the casket. Most of the pallbearers would also be Corner gang members. I would be one of them helping carry Charlie to his grave. I did the same with my father. It is a proud feeling, but not a pleasant feeling.

The room was loaded with flowers, and Charlie looked great. Undertakers are like taxidermists. Some of them can make a trout look like a trout and some of them can make a trout look like a walrus. The undertakers in Lawrence were obviously craftsmen. With my dad, Mr. Rosinski took dad's wedding picture, and made my father look like he must have looked when he was twenty years old. He really and truly looked better dead than he did alive. Charlie was the same. Mr. Breen must have taken Charlie's high school graduation picture, and Charlie was once again a dapper dude. Everything was perfect, from the eyebrows to the combed and brushed eyelashes. His cheeks all red and his lips all rosy and he was dead as a doornail.

The corpse looked so alive that some people had to reach out and touch it, just to make sure. I had done that with my father. The back of his hand was as cold as ice. I didn't have any need to touch Charlie. By this time I could accept the fact of death and what it looked like.

Periodically each of us would rise from our front row seat and go up and stand next to Charlie. Some would kneel on the kneeler and say a prayer or something. I just looked. I decided rather than talk to God about the whole situation that I would just talk to Charlie. I told him that I hoped that his gamble had come out to his advantage. I had asked him one Friday when he was going to confession if he really believed in all that hocus pocus. He said that he really didn't know, but being in the position that he was in, why take the chance. So he said his "bless me Fathers" and his "Hail Marys" and "Our Fathers." He dropped his coins in the box, lit a candle on the altar each week and went to mass every Sunday. So if there is a heaven Charlie should be up there looking for a butt tray so that he doesn't have to crush his Luckies on God's streets of gold. Knowing Charlie he is probably F B I-ing the whole damn place anyway. I visualized him up there pitching pennies up against one of heaven's walls. I imagine that heaven must have walls, don't you? What are the Golden Gates attached to, otherwise?

I could see and hear Charlie clicking his leather heals up to the confessional. I could see his face when Niki started squirming in his lap. I could see him slapping his cigarette packs against his palm; or leaning up against the cottage sink; or sitting in the old Bishop's with his lobster bib on and sucking up that lobster tail dripping with butter; or standing at the comic book rack at Walter's in his tux; or in his altar boy outfit downstairs in the basement under the Church puffing on a butt. I had known Charlie forever.

I wasn't angry about anything. Only believers can be angry. They have somebody to blame. I could find no more blame. There was only, "now you see him, now you don't" like peek-a-boo and hide and seek. It is just all fun and games.

We all sat there in the front row like little statues. Nobody cried. Charlie's mom and dad didn't know half of the people who came in the front door. Whenever they saw a face that they didn't recognize, they ran over to one of us. Is that boy or girl, or person one of yours ... one of Charlie's chums? Invariably it was, and we would jump up. We quickly became part of the greeting squad. This was once again a proud feeling. We were like a part of the Kareckas family. We were wanted, needed and appreciated. This was very satisfying to a bunch of street kids who had spent their lives being chased from one corner to another by the cops and all our good neighbors, of course. Who the hell wanted us ... any of us?

Everybody came to see Charlie. Even the team from the Y showed up - John the Thinker, Harry the Walker, even Mister America. When Mister America knelt down on the bench there was no room for anybody else.

Originally we thought that we would just go to the wake on the first day; stay an hour or two; then show up Sunday for the funeral. But as the day progressed we saw that there would be no leaving for any of us. We were functionaries. We showed up morning, noon and night for the next three days, and stood our posts. We mixed and mingled. We introduced people to the Kareckas family. We went back into the kitchen area and had coffee and smoked cigarettes, and told stories and listened to others tell their stories. We visited with Charlie, F B I-ed the area and kept everything "ship shape."

Helen came in looking like a lost waif who had been out selling apples on some street corner. She looked bad - not ugly or poorly dressed or anything like that, just distraught. Charlie's mom and dad didn't know Helen from a hole in the wall. At first she didn't want to meet Charlie's parents, but I made her follow me. I didn't say anything about this being Charlie's girl friend or anything. I just said that this was one of the young ladies that Charlie and the rest of us met down at the Cottage and had befriended.

When she went over and took a look at Charlie in the box, her knees quaked and I had to grab her under one arm and prop her up. I told her to kneel down on the prayer rail until she got her strength back.

Soldiers always talk about war, but just plain, old, everyday death is hardship enough for me. I don't really need all the bombs, bullets or blood to make me feel any worse. A simple, old-fashioned, un-mangled, manicured corpse is horrible enough as far as I can see. I get the idea, thank-you.

Death is a phenomenon. Love is a phenomenon. Life is a curiosity, but nothing any of us should take too, too seriously.

Of all of the events of that summer with Charlie, this wake stands out most in my mind. There was something about sitting there in that front row everyday staring at Charlie laid out in a box. It wasn't so shocking seeing him dead. I had pictured him that way a million times over the last several months. Ever since my father died I pictured everybody dead. I used to visualize each of my friends laid out in a casket with a pair of rosary beads in their hands. It was kind of like when you first discovered sex. You start picturing everybody naked, your mother your father, everybody. It is kind of normal, I would guess. I had no particular desire to hang around funeral parlors or mortuaries, or see if I could create my own personal corpses. I just visualized live people as dead, every once in awhile. None of them ever ended up dead three days later either. It was just one of those mental abortions, or whatever.

Us guys staying at the funeral parlor from beginning to end was just the frosting on the cake. We had been assigned the dying body of Chucky for the last months of his life, and now we would watch over and protect the corpse until we put it into the ground. We were his guardian angels here on earth. Maybe he will be able to help us out on the other end.

The funeral was a military funeral. All that means is that at the grave site, five or six guys show up and shoot some rifles and drape an American flag over the casket. It adds a touch.

My sister and I were mad at my Uncle Joe's funeral. We were mad at my dad and all of his buddies because they did so much celebrating at the hall after the body had been dumped into a hole somewhere. My father tried to explain all the celebrating that next day after he sobered up. His explanation didn't really hold up. We thought that they had all acted disgracefully and we were right.

Charlie's casket really didn't seem all that heavy. We slipped a pack of Lucky Strikes and his porkpie hat into the casket when nobody was watching just before they closed it up. Seeing the casket being closed up is another one of those not so good memories. But we were all proud to be there until the very end. Friends to the end for our little buddy.

That next weekend at Salisbury Beach, I went over to St. Ann's. I went to confession. I put a couple of bucks into the box and lit a couple of candles, just like Charlie had done every weekend. For twenty bucks I bought him some masses. At the end or in the middle of the mass some place, the priest steps forward and says; "This mass is dedicated to the repose of the souls of Charles Kareckas, Bob Jones and Pete Rugalo." So I bought twenty bucks worth of those. That Sunday I went to mass and communion, and that must have filled me up. Since that summer, over forty years ago, I have never felt the craving for such an experience ever again. I haven't been back.

On the other hand, I still love Maine Lobster. Whenever I eat one, I tell everybody at the table about how much my little buddy Charlie from the old neighborhood used to love them. He was the one who got me started on those things. And sometimes, occasionally, I have the overwhelming desire to pick up a cigarette butt lying on the sidewalk someplace. When I do, I always check to see if it's a Lucky Strike. When it is, I think to myself ... That's my buddy Chucky, just saying hello. And then I see

Charlie, standing out on the sidewalk in front of the gates to heaven, hanging on a corner, sporting his porkpie hat and pounding a pack of unopened butts onto his palm.

"What the hell you doin' up there Charlie?"

"Nothing much, Richie. Just waitin' on the rest of you guys. Bring a deck of cards will you? Hey, you'll never guess ... I think I saw Harry the Walker yesterday."

"No kidding?"

When I was little, I had a
    friend.
We said we would be friends,
    until the end.
We didn't lie.
And when he died,
I cried...
and I cried
and I cried.

HANGIN' OUT

We're hangin' out. There's Jack, Jim, Dick, and Chuck.
There's Grecsey and the Coze.
We're hangin' out.
We're shootin' a few hoops down at the school yard.
There's Burnsey with the swisher.
The swisher that is never a misser, but always a swisher.
And there's B.J. with the steal.
We're over Costy's playin' a little tag-rush.
We're hangin' out ma, just hangin' out.
Where ya goin' son?
I'm goin' out. Down the Corner. Just hangin' out.

We're playin' a little Forty-fives,
Or just tossin' pennies up to the wall.
We're listening to old Walter.
He's down the Red Sox summer camp tryin' out.
We got phosphate, sarsaparilla, lime rickey, all Curran
      and Joyce.
We got potato chips from the Granite State,
All wrapped in a silver bag.
We got sheet-paper candy, nigger babies,
And sweet rock on a string.
We're hangin' out ma, just hangin' out.
We're over Nell's givin' 'em hell,
Sittin' on their curb, or up on their steps.
We're bouncin' a ball off Alma Meter's wall.
We're havin' fun ... until the cops come.
Then it's time for a little walk around the block.

We're hangin' out ma, just hangin' out.

It's winter time.
We're hoppin' cars.
We're hangin' in hallways.
We're down the English Social settin' up duck pins.
We're at Liggett's drinkin' hot chocolate.
We got Walter talkin' about World War II.
It's snowin' and blowin' and we're hopin' he never gets
        through.
We're down the Corner, we're hangin' out.
We're just hangin' out ma, just hangin' out.

There's a screech and a skid and a mashin' of gears.
There goes a car slippin' and slidin' and kickin' up dirt.
Old Walter is at the window throwin' up his hands;
"That's Dobson! He'll be on a slab ...
On a slab. I'll tell ya, he'll be on a slab."
We're hangin' out ma, just hangin' out.
We're down on the Corner, we're hangin' out.

We're up at the Howard Playstead.
We're on the park bench.
Willie says that he needs just two more cents.
We're spittin' in the sewer.
We're watchin' the cars.
We're layin' up on the hill.
We're lookin' at the stars.
Hey, there goes Joe's sister, Betty, in her new
        tight sweater.
Man oh man, life's just gettin' better and better.
We're hangin' out ma, just hangin' out.
I'm goin' up to the Corner ma, just gonna hang out.

We can listen to Russ.
He's in love again.
"She the kind of girl who likes to darn socks.
She makes biscuits and cakes and homemade bread.
She has those eyes; the kind that make you want to cry.
And when she sighs, God, I nearly die."
What's her name Russ?
"Oh, I think it's Sherry. No, no ... it's Terry.
No, that's not right.
It's? Oh ya ... it's Fay ... Fay Berry."

We're hangin' out ma. We're just hangin' out.
We're goin' to the Corner.
We're hangin' out.
It's Friday night, and we're goin' to the dance.
We're goin' to Rock and Roll and look for romance.
We're goin' to give Central Catholic just one more chance.
We're gonna be cool.
We're gonna slick down the old D. A. with some Charles
        Antell.
It's got lanolin, wow!
We're hangin' out ma, We're just hangin' out.

Tonight we're goin' to get Togie to get us some brew.
He's sixteen but looks twenty-two.
A quart of Black Label or a G.I.Q.
A couple of pizzas and a meat filled pie.
If Togie can't do it, we'll find old Billy.
We'll go to Cronin's and get Billy the Bum,
Or maybe one of his chums.
We'll buy him a pint or maybe a quart,
We'll promise not to tell, even if we get caught.
We're hangin' out ma, just hangin' out.
It's Sunday morning. It's mass at King Tut's;
Vanilla Cokes, red pistachio fingers.

Dutch is readin' over at the rack.
Grecs wants to go to church.
He wants to watch the girls.
He wants to ouu and aww and dream of playin' with their
        curls.
A nickel in the juke box,
Listen to Fats and The Elvis sway and swing.
Or maybe somebody will play "My Ding-a-ling."
We're hangin' out ma, we're just hangin' out.

Hey, let's take a little walk down to the Y.
We'll play sidewalk tennis or shoot a little pool;
Maybe some checkers?
We'll see Harry the Walker, General Mills, or John the
        Thinker.
Somebody will yell BOOM, and we'll all be gone.
We're hangin' out ma, just hangin' out.

We're goin' down to Kap's; its Tuesday night.
We'll stare at all the girls and get 'em up tight.
Then maybe over to King Size, or Lawton's by the Sea for
A dog or two on a grilled, buttered bun.
Then go for a walk, or maybe back up to the Howard.
We're hangin' out ma, just hangin' out.
We ain't doin' nothing; just sittin' on the wall; hangin'
        out.

Today it's sunny; we might thumb to the beach.
Fried clams, onion rings, lamb on a stick;
A trip to the arcade; a walk on the beach.
We'll go down to the Black Rocks; buy us a Foam.
Then before it gets dark we'll thumb on back home.
We're hangin' out ma, just hangin' out.
We're up the Corner, just hangin' out.

It don't matter the time of the day.
There will always be someone goin' up that way.
You can play if you want, or just sit on the bench.
There's never a hassle, there's always a joke.
There's always someone to listen.
You may be right, you may be wrong,
But, nevertheless, you'll always belong.
Sometimes you'll find a new point of view.
Just something that Pete, Red, or Gerry might have said
With a grin or a smile.
It was a long, long time ... a long, long time
That we were all kids, just one of the guys.
Just hangin' out, sittin' up on the wall.
Just hangin' out ma, just hangin' out.

Sometimes we were just there.
Sometimes it was a ball.
Now I'm older and that's all the past.
Often I wonder if it is my memory's lapse,
Or did I really know any of those guys.
We're they really pals, buddies, friends?
Their memory gets fuzzy.
I tell myself that there is only today.
They never knew me and I never knew them.
They're just a bunch of ghosts in my memory's way.
But then when I'm huddled in one of those lonely
        corners,
With all the dark shadows, hard knuckles and calloused
        hearts,
I hear a sigh, a creak, a crack, a cry,
And then there is a tear in my eye.
I see a laughing face, then feel a slap on my back.
It could be Tom or Dutch, Chuck or Jack.
And all of a sudden,
I'm up on the Corner. I'm on the wall.

I'm hangin' out ma, just hangin' out.
I'm on the Corner.
I'm in Costy's yard.
I'm down at Nell's,
Or in Michaud's back seat.
I'm up Joe's cellar;
Or behind the English Social, a little stickball.
Or down the beach.
I'm just standin' on the Corner,
Or in the middle of Lawrence Street.
I'm hangin' out ma.
I'm just hangin' out with my friends, my buddies.
Up on the Corner,
Hangin' out ma, just hangin' out.
I'm up the Corner.
I'm on that old bench.
I'm with my old buddies.
I'm hangin' out ma, just hangin' out.
...I'm just hangin' out.

Richard Edward Noble

NOW SOMETHING MORE

HISTORICAL NOTE
The Bread and Roses Strike of 1912   *page 117*

LAWRENCE-MY HOMETOWN
A taste of what's to come   *page 131*

HAVE YOU READ THESE BOOKS
Also by Richard Edward Noble   *page 145*

MEET THE AUTHOR
Richard Edward Noble   *page 153*

HISTORICAL NOTE

The Bread and Roses strike of 1912 was a major historical event in the history and evolution of Lawrence, Massachusetts. It should be common knowledge to all Lawrencians. The following historical essay is my small contribution to achieving that goal.

Bread and Roses Strike of 1912

On Tuesday, January 11, 1912 in the industrial mill town of Lawrence Massachusetts, a group of Polish immigrant women who were working at the Everett Mills on Union Street, shut down their machines and walked off the job. Within hours 25,000 co-workers had joined them in what would become the biggest textile strike that had ever been staged in America.

Lawrence, Massachusetts was a planned community built specifically for the textile industry in 1845. Its main attraction was the availability of water power, primarily the Merrimack River and its many tributaries. Like its sister city down the river, Lowell, it was going to be a utopian village designed on the model of New Lanark, established in Scotland by the social reformer Robert Owen. But, by the year 1912, the dream had faded. Far from being an industrial paradise, both Lawrence and Lowell by the year 1912 were considered by many to be "industrial blots, pestiferous and diseased," sustained on the starving, over-worked backs of women and children. The mill owners had evolved in sixty some years, from humanitarian and utopian idealists to Robber Barons.

Lawrence, known as the "Immigrant City" was at the time of the Bread and Roses Strike about 85,000 strong. Thirty-seven percent of that 85,000 had arrived in the previous ten years. Most had been lured to the area by advertisements abroad, placed by mill agents, touting streets of gold and money and jobs in abundance for everyone. More than half the population of Lawrence was directly involved in mill work. The population breakdown went something as follows; 21,000 Irish, 12,000 Franco American, 8000, Italians, 6,000 Germans, 3,000 Lithuanians, 2,700 Syrians, 2,500 European Jews, 2,300 Scots, and a small group of blacks who had settled there after the Civil War. There were only 3,000 of its 85,000 residents that were born in the United States.

Many notables visiting the Lawrence area were shocked by the conditions of squalor and poverty. Elizabeth Shapleigh, a physician, had conducted a mortality study. She found that every third person standing in her line in Lawrence was dying from tuberculosis directly related to dust and fiber and breathing conditions at the mills. One third of the mill workers died before the age of twenty-five, and a large number of children who had started working in the mills before becoming teenagers didn't survive their teenage years.

Seventy-five percent of the workers in the Lawrence mills, ended up dying from mill related causes. The average mill worker earned about $9.00 a week. The average rent was $3.00 per week. Most workers were barely getting by, many were starving.

The tenements were stacking people up, six hundred to the acre. At Fall River sixteen tenements housed 500 human beings. They had one privy. In Lowell the tenants had to carry their garbage and excrement to a deposit station. Miscarriages were everyday. Conditions in Manchester, New Hampshire were said to be even worse than the horror reported in the working class neighborhoods of Manchester, England. American workers started working at an earlier age and died a decade sooner.

A worker could be fined 25 cents for being five minutes late; one dollar for eating at the loom; 25 cents for taking time to wash one's hands, doing inadequate work, sitting down or taking a drink of water. Some mill owners charged the workers for drinking water.

Paydays were often irregular. An employee might wait 50 days to finally get paid for thirty. In some New England areas some workers were paid in company script redeemable at company stores. It was common practice to lock workers in their working area rooms. Crippling injuries were common place and incurable diseases precipitated by working conditions were everywhere.

Camella Teoli testified before congress about working conditions in the mills. Miss Teoli was barely a teenager when her hair was caught in one of the machines and her scalp was ripped off. She spent seven months in the hospital recuperating … without pay.

Most kids worked in the mills and didn't attend school. On an average day in New Jersey, of children registered for classes, you could count on over a million absentees. The ratio was, most likely, similar for Lawrence. Just up the road from Lawrence, in North Andover, mill owners were paying the "better class workers" who were of Irish, Scotch and English descent, double the wages of the more recent, Polish, Lithuanian, Syrian, French Canadian and Slave immigrant mill workers in Lawrence.

The state legislature had finally stepped in to try and assist the desperate and helpless women and children working in the mills. They passed a law limiting women, and children under sixteen, to a maximum of 54 hours per week. This was a two hour reduction from the previous average of 56 hours per week. The mill owners obeyed the law but added a touch or two of their own. Since the mills could not run without the women and children who comprised over 50% of the worker population, they cut all worker hours to 54. They increased the production so that the same output would be accomplished in the shorter hours. And they deducted two hours pay from everyone's pay checks. Naturally they were not going to pay people for working 56 hours when they had only worked 54.

At the same time the American Woolen Company, the largest group of mills in the area, was paying its share holders 12% on their investment. Shares that had been bought at $75 were worth $3,800 in just a few years. William "Billy" Wood who owned American Woolen claimed to have so many automobiles that he couldn't keep track of them. In 1910 the American Woolen Company announced profits of $3,995,000.

The Wood Mill was built in 1906. Each of the wings of its main building stretched for a half mile along the Merrimack River and canals. Wood also owned the Ayer, the Washington and the Prospect. Eventually, he owned mills all over the nation.

Billy Wood began his career as an office boy in the Wamsutta Cotton Mills in New Bedford. At age twenty-eight he went to the Washington Mills in Lawrence. He became a salesman for the company and by 1880 was earning $25,000 a year. His fortunes continued to grow, especially after marring Mr. Ayer's daughter.

The American Woolen Company had thirteen thousand employees, itself. Lawrence was the worsted capital of the world. It was stated that Lawrence "weaved the worsteds for the world." Worsted is made from weaving wool not cotton.

At the time of the Lawrence strike 400,000 men, women and children worked in the Textile mills of New England. The Boston Associates, the Essex Company, the American Woolen Company and a few other investment trusts were comprised of some of the richest men in America.

The two hour cut in pay amounted to just 32 cents. But 32 cents could buy a worker between three and ten loaves of bread.

"We will break this strike," Lawrence mayor Scanlon announced, "or we will break the strikers' heads."

On Saturday, January 13, strike organizers Joseph Ettor and Arturo Giovannetti from the I.W.W., Industrial Workers of the World, arrived. Scanlon called Governor Eugene Foss, a mill owner himself, for state troops. Five hundred soldiers were immediately sent into the city. Students from Harvard University were given extra credit toward their final exams to go down, and "have a fling at those people." Harvard University president at that time was A. Lawrence Lowell.

Four days after the strike began most mills had armed guards and mill owners were advertising for "scabs." The natives who were for the most part Irish, didn't participate in the strike. Father James O'Reilly of St. Mary's Church who had in the past been a supporter of the mill workers spoke out against the strike. The Catholic Church did not like the socialist-communist-atheistic I.W.W. Some of the workers at the mills were represented by the United Textile Workers. Their leader was John Golden. Golden and Samuel Gompers of the A.F of L. spoke out against the I.W.W. and their infamous leader, "one eyed" Big Bill Haywood. Both Golden and Gompers headed unions that supported craftsmen only. Both groups had been called upon in the past to intercede for mill workers, but were always a no-show.

The I.W.W. supported laborers as well as craftsmen, blacks as well as whites, and women. The A.F.L. did not support the strike and Golden actually advised his members to break the picket lines and go back to work.

Though most English speaking workers and members of the craft unions did not support the strike, they didn't break the picket lines. They simply stayed home and didn't report for work. The A.F.L., the United Textile Workers, the Catholic Church, local priests, the Irish, and native born English speaking Lawrencians didn't support the strike. But on January 24 when Big Bill Haywood and Elizabeth Gurley Flynn made their first appearance two weeks into the strike, over fifteen thousand mill workers greeted them down at the Common, a fifteen acre park, in the center of the town. It was said to be the largest gathering in the history of Lawrence.

Although the churches, and craft unions, and others didn't support the strike, many did help in setting up soup kitchens and providing general aid to the strikers. The mill owners hired guards, strike breakers and hoodlums to instigate violence and stir up trouble that could be blamed on the workers. The strike leaders advised the workers to refrain from violence, because if blood is shed, it will most likely be your own, they were told.

Mayor Scanlon made further requests for troop support from Governor Foss. One thousand two hundred National Guardsmen were sent in. They housed themselves in the mills, set up searchlights and placed machine guns on the factory's roof tops. The bosses had also installed electric-wire fences and armed loyal employees. Lawrence was a city under siege.

On January 15 eight thousand strikers marched through a snow storm to stop "scabs" from entering the Washington and Wood mills. By the time the strikers got to the Prospect Mill they were fifteen thousand in number. At the Atlantic and Pacific mills the militia finally stopped them with high pressure fire hoses. At another gathering National Guardsmen waded into the crowd and the strikers had their first death. A young Syrian youth, about twenty years of age, by the name of John Ramey was bayoneted in the back. He spent two weeks in the hospital and then died.

The Bread and Roses strike of 1912 goes down into the history books for a number of reasons. One was because of the prominent part played in it by women. Helen Gurly Flynn, originally from Concord New Hampshire was, as mentioned, a major force in the I.W.W. But there was a heap of others; Josephine Lis, Annie Welzenback, Sarah Bagley, Jennie Collins and Mary Kerney O'Sullivan to mention but a few. But the regular working women and working mothers were the real heroes.

Prosecutor Douglas Campbell commented, "It takes but one man to overcome ten men, but it requires ten men to manage a single woman." The women laid down on the sidewalks and in the streets. They were pushed, shoved and clubbed. Police Chief John J. Sullivan defended the violence of his bullying patrolmen by stating that the women had it coming to them. Headlines in the local newspapers read, humiliatingly; Man intimidated by women pickets; Woman fined 20 dollars for assaulting and officer; Jennie Radsiarlowitz convicted for intimidating man. Finally the police outdid themselves in the most shocking embarrassment of all.

Due to the growing escalation in violence, striking parents, at the suggestion of union leaders, decided to send their small children away from the area. It was Washington's Birthday. The small children being packed off at the train station created such a stir of sympathetic, union publicity that marshals declared such action illegal.

Colonel Sweeter of the National Guard had placed Lawrence virtually under marshal law. They charged the parents with "neglect." One hundred and fifty children had been sent to New York and Margaret Sanger, later to become famous as organizer of the National Birth Control

125

League, organized the committee to supervise the children.

News of the Lawrence strike spawned huge demonstrations in support of the strikers in London, Rome, Bern and Budapest. On Saturday, February 24 the women of Lawrence defied the Marshal's order and brought more of their children down to the train station on Broadway. When the women tried to put their children onto the train the police waded into them with their billy clubs. They struck children and women alike. Bertha Crouse, a pregnant striker, was clubbed into unconsciousness and consequently lost her baby.

In another incident Annie Lopizzo was shot and killed. Witnesses said that it was policeman Oscar Benoit who had done the killing. Benoit had been stabbed and immediately began shooting into the crowd.

The police arrested Joseph Caruso as the murderer, then picked up Ettor and Geovannitti as accessories. Ettor and Geovannetti were accessories because they were the leaders of the "illegal strike conspiracy," organized in restraint of trade and the obstruction of private property rights, as outlined in the Sherman Anti-trust Act.

Neither man was present at the scene of the crime. Caruso, as it turns out, was not present at the scene of the crime, either. But the three men were not lonely at the city jail and elsewhere. Hundreds of strikers, many of them women, had been arrested and were cooling their heels with broken bones and busted heads.

Helen Keller came to Lawrence and spoke out in favor of the release of Ettor and Geovannetti. A stash of dynamite had also showed up, mysteriously, in a shoe store next to where Joseph Ettor picked up his mail.

An investigation ensued and Ettor and Giovannetti were cleared of any "dynamite" charges when it was discovered that an ex-alderman and son of a former mayor by the name of John Breen had actually planted the dynamite in the shoe store himself. This admission of guilt was prompted from Mr. Breen when it was discovered that he had wrapped the dynamite in a subscription magazine or newspaper with his name and address printed on the material.

All this negative publicity caused "Captain Billy" Wood to have a change of heart. He offered the workers a 5% wage increase even though the company, according to him, was going through stressful times and making nothing in terms of profit.

A few days later it was announced that American Woolen had a surplus of 11.5 million and would be paying dividends to its shareholders of 8%. Captain Billy was also charged in the dynamite conspiracy. Supposedly, Wood had hired Breen to do the dirty work. Breen had an unexplainable payment receipt from Mr. Wood in his possession. Breen was eventually fined $500 for his part in the shenanigans. The charges against Captain Billy were dismissed. Ettor and Geovannetti remained in jail even after the strike was settled.

After two months the strike finally ended. All the negative publicity; the beating of the women and children at the train station; the beating and forced abortion of Burtha Crouse; the killings of Anna Lopizzo and John Ramy; the dynamite affair and the Breen confession; the unexplained check paid to Breen from Billy Wood; all these events had undermined the mill owners' objectives. They gave the workers pay raises between 10% and 20%; they hired strikers back without reprisals; and they eliminated their corrupt piecework practices.

The Bread and Roses Strike not only sent shivers throughout the local business community, but it panicked mill owners throughout the nation. Textile workers and industrial workers all over the nation received wage increases. The Bread and Roses Strike in Lawrence, Massachusetts goes down in the history books as a turning point in labor management relations. Nevertheless, many strikers who were imprisoned and charged unconstitutionally, without trial or representation, were forgotten in their jail cells. Some remained in jail for up to two years.

Ettor and Geovannetti remained in jail also. The charge of conspiracy and accessories to murder remained against them. The penalty was death. Big Bill Haywood immediately organized the mill workers on the two men's behalf. In September a grand jury secretly indicted Haywood and several other strike leaders under similar charges. Haywood left Massachusetts. After eight months of postponements the state finally set a date for the trial, September 30.

On September 15, 1912 there was to be a rally on behalf of Ettor and Geovannetti on the Boston Common. Rumor had it that Haywood was going to sneak into town and make a speech at the rally. The Boston Police were alerted. Big Bill made his appearance successfully. He gave a riveting speech to a crowd of over twenty thousand workers. Haywood demanded that Ettor and Geovannetti be released, if not, a strike would be re-established. The jail doors would open or the mill doors would close, chanted Haywood.

After his speech, Haywood inadvertently slipped into the back seat of a waiting unmarked police car instead of his getaway car. He was arrested and booked. What was he being charged with, the newspaper men asked him. "They tell me I'm charged with conspiracy. I don't really know what kind of conspiracy but I think it is a conspiracy to get more to eat."

Haywood was now on trial once again for his life. The plot failed. In a trial that took place in Salem,

Massachusetts, charges were dropped for lack of evidence and all four men were finally released after eleven months of negotiating.

The victory of the belligerent and warlike I.W.W. sent mill owners and industrialists running to more accommodating and sympathetic union organizations. The A.F.L., the United Textile Workers and others had a line of businessmen at their doors. Many businessmen even solicited the more non-violent unions to come in and organize their workers. The times, they were a changing.

LAWRENCE - MY HOMETOWN

A Taste of What's to Come

Lawrence – My Hometown *is a book of humorous tales and old "war" stories about growing up in Lawrence, Massachusetts in the 40s, 50s and 60s. Look for it soon on Amazon.com, the world's largest internet bookseller or at your local bookstore. Buy direct and save from Noble Publishing. Contact richardedwardnoble@fairpoint.net.*

The following are three typical vignettes.

Clarence Darrow, F. Lee Bailey and Morris Ravitch

I have written about this event in my mini-novel A Summer with Charlie, but now here's "the rest of the story."

The Salisbury police busted into our little castle on Old Towne Way and threw a bunch of us into the pokey. Those of us who were the victims of this brutality on the part of the Salisbury police decided that we would take this group of ruffians to court. After all, we were all mature, responsible adults at the time of our arrest and it was unanimous that these make believe, wannabe flatfoots had grossly overstepped their authority. Who did they think they were dealing with here - a bunch of kids? So what if we had a few beers and were a little rowdy, we were old enough to drink – most of us. We paid for our booze. We paid our cottage rent. We contributed to the financial success of the 5 O'clock Club, and the Normandy, and the Kon Tiki, Mac Jenney's, the Edward's Hotel and the Bowery and everywhere man! We were a positive attribute of the Salisbury economic community. We should have been treated with some respect! We weren't a bunch of punk kids sitting out on the corner no more. We were adults and should be treated accordingly. We worked for a living. We collected paychecks. We were big boys now. We had this same cottage for the last three years in a row. We didn't get thrown out. The place had not been condemned or anything like that. We decided to contest our fines and seek damages for being abused, mistreated, manhandled, harassed, and humiliated. We got a court date.

In the weeks before our day in court, we decided to solicit character witnesses from our beach neighborhood on Old Towne Way. Most of the neighbors agreed that we had not caused a disturbance on the night in question. Of course, many of them were guys we knew who were also from Lawrence or Lowell or Haverhill and had rented their own cottage. Nevertheless a number of them agreed to come and testify on our behalf.

This was all well and good but we needed a "credible" witness. There was good old George and his family who lived across the way and a few doors down. He was a nice guy. We had him and his wife over to our place many times for a beer and some pizza or an Italian hoagie from Lena's or Tony's (Pappalardo's) Subs. He was not only a real person but also a retired cop from Haverhill. We decided to go over and talk to him about our situation.

When we told him that we had been arrested for disturbing the peace he was shocked. He was right there in his cottage that night and he never heard a thing.

"Would you come to court and testify for us, George?"

"You are darn right, I will! These guys down here aren't even real police. They're a bunch of part-time bozos who want to be important. I don't know how they get off arresting you guys."

"All right, George!"

When our day in court finally arrived, we gathered up all our buddies and went and got George. As we wandered, nervously around the court house, who do we bump into? Why, none other than the most famous barrister in all of Lawrence, Morris Ravitch.

When Morris found out that we were defending ourselves in this endeavor. He shook his head sadly and said, "That could be a big mistake, boys. You know the old saying; A man who is his own defense often ends up with a fool for his attorney. If I were you guys, I wouldn't go in there without a lawyer."

"Yeah, but we can't afford no lawyer."

"What the heck are you talking about? How many accused do we have here?"

"There's six of us."

"Okay, you got ten bucks each?" We all began shuffling through our billfolds and we each gave Morris ten bucks.

"Okay boys, you're all set. I'll see you in court."

"Don't you need to know about our case?"

"Oh yeah, what happened to you guys anyway?"

We told Morris our whole story and introduced him to George and all the rest of our witnesses.

The Salisbury cops gave their side of the story first: We were loud and noisy. All the neighbors had been calling. We were all drunks. We were out in the middle of the street waving beer bottles around. We were sitting on top of cars. We were yelling and screaming and using abusive language. We had the radio blearing. There were half naked, underage girls everywhere, and yeahti, yeahti, yeahti – the same old same old we had heard a million times.

We were all dressed in our Sunday best. One by one we told the judge of the physical and psychological abuse that had scarred our personalities – probably for the rest of our lives. We showed the judge the marks still on our wrists from the handcuffs. We contested the drunken issue and why shouldn't girls be half naked – this was Salisbury Beach for god's sake. Everybody is half naked at the beach. If any of the girls were under age they weren't under by much and they had never mentioned it to any of us. Yes we may have been sitting on cars but they were our cars, parked in our parking spaces. But we took a special exception to the noise accusation. At this point Morris started calling the neighbors to testify.

The judge didn't seem to be buying a word of it until Morris brought up old George, the retired Haverhill policeman. The Judge even knew George. Morris asked

George if he had heard the aforementioned social disturbance.

"I'll tell ya, I didn't hear a thing. These kids are all great. I live right across the street. I have even been over to their cottage. These are all good boys."

"You didn't hear a lot of screaming and yelling?"

"I didn't hear anything."

"You didn't hear anything?" Morris emphasized. "You live right across the street and you didn't hear any noise? You didn't hear the alleged loud music? You didn't hear boys and girls screaming and yelling?"

"Nothing! I didn't hear anything."

"My god, are you deaf or what?" one of the accusing cops burst from his seat."

"Well," George said. "I have been having a little trouble lately. The doctor says that my right ear is completely gone but my left ear is still working at about 50 percent. I don't hear everything these days. I have to keep the TV volume up pretty high. But I'm getting by."

The judge fined each of us forty bucks apiece. We didn't get any jail time though. Thank-you Mr. Morris Ravitch, attorney at law.

Okay Boys, Back Off and Spread Out!

A Summer with Charlie is a rather short book. It is actually a long short story. While writing it I tried to keep the focus of the book on Charlie and his life situation and not get lost recording the various antics of the infamous Howard Ass - as Ray Dolan had dubbed the old corner gang. Consequently there was more left out of the book about that fateful summer than actually went into the book. Here's one that didn't make the cut.

After a rather ruckus weekend at Old Towne Way and everybody had disappeared back to the city and the real world of 9 to 5, Charlie and I were left to clean up the disaster. Charlie relished this duty. I don't know why, but he would scurry around in his pork pie hat and bathing suit with broom or mop in hand whistling and humming all morning. I suppose if I didn't have such a terrible hangover every Monday morning, I would have found this comforting rather than annoying.

The first thing that we discovered was that somebody had broken the commode in our unique back porch toilet.

The bathroom sat on the back porch of our cottage. Hang a right after exiting the kitchen, take about fifteen paces and there was a door. The average homeowner would probably conclude that the door to this shelter hid a utility room or a storage closet, but it contained the toilet and a bathroom sink.

Being rather unhandy, I was under the impression that commodes were another of those mysteries provided by God in his infinite goodness – a divine intervention of sorts. Commodes always were and always would be, thank-you God, amen.

That is not the case. Commodes are manmade. Right there in this little hardware store in the town of Salisbury sat a variety of commodes for sale.

We installed the new commode and put the old one on the back porch a few paces from the kitchen door. We would take it to the dump with all the empty beer, wine and hard liquor bottles the Monday following this weekend's fiasco.

For this weekend's agenda we had a new idea – we would concoct a "punch" for the girls. Girls dig punch and we figured that it would add an air of class to the joint. Besides, everybody was drinking up all the Seagram's 7, Smirnoff Vodka, Bacardi Rum, Beefeater Gin and our prized Kruger beer in the little ugly Kruger bottles.

The more we thought about this punch the more involved it got. We wanted to put a large amount of hard liquor in our punch, of course. Girls need a good shot or two before they can loosen up. But girls are also very cautious. They don't want to get too loose - which means that the potency of the punch has to be disguised in some way or other. Then there was the expense. We always had lots of company and strangers can suck up a good quantity of free punch.

We bought several quart bottles of booze that came under the Shamrock logo. Shamrock? It was about a quarter the price of any booze that was for real. It was horrible, but we had a plan.

We bought one quart of Shamrock scotch, one quart of Shamrock gin, one quart of Shamrock rum, one quart of Shamrock vodka, and one quart of Shamrock Irish whisky. But now we needed something to make all this booze taste like Kool-aide. We bought two gallons of sweet Cucamonga wine, several large cans of fruit cocktail and various other fruits, a few cans of Dole pineapple rings to float on the top, and six large cans of Hawaiian Punch. I suppose in today's world this could be construed to be the original date rape drug.

We went to a used kitchen supply store and got a bunch of "punch glasses" for about two cents each. They weren't very dainty. They were all different colors and had nice handles on them but they probably held a full cup of liquid each. We thought one cup per dip of punch was just about right.

We couldn't find the right sized punch bowl though. Then somebody suggested that we use the kitchen sink. It was a good sized, old-fashioned, deep, dishwashing sized sink. What a great idea!

Shortly before things got rolling that Saturday night we prepared the sink for the punch. A few of the guys used the sink that morning to shave. Consequently there were a ton of little hairs sticking to the white porcelain bowl. We had nine guys and only one bathroom - some facial hair in the kitchen sink was to be expected. We cleaned it – a little. We bought new sink stoppers and made sure that the sink did not leak. We didn't want all our efforts washing down the drain.

We dumped all the booze into the kitchen sink punch bowl and then gradually added Cucamonga wine, canned fruit and Hawaiian Punch until the taste of the Shamrock liquor was undetectable. That took all the Hawaiian Punch, all the Cucamonga wine, and all the canned fruit. The canned fruit and the floating pineapple rings did add a very nice touch.

When the girls started wandering in, it was mandatory that they be escorted by one of the house "chaperones" over to the sink for a try at the punch. [We thought of ourselves more as guardian angels than as chaperones.] All the girls loved the punch. It was so sweet and "yummy."

"Is there much liquor in here?" she would ask, naively.

"Noooo, it is mostly fruit and Hawaiian Punch," one of us cottage angels would advise.

Well, I am gonna tell you, the girls loosened up pretty quick after a couple of "tiny" cups of that hobo style Hawaiian Punch.

The first cup would only be a quarter full for most girls. But after awhile they wound be stumbling over one another to that sink laughing, giggling and slopping up those cups to the brim. By the fourth or fifth cup of Hobo Punch the girls were bobbing for fruit cocktail cherries and getting pineapple rings caught on their noses.

Actually we had over done it. A few hours at our punch bowl and most of the girls weren't good for anything – even a little idle conversation was difficult.

For example, me and Charlie were cooling off out on the back porch having a cigarette. The interior of the cottage was jammed. A girl suddenly came tumbling out the kitchen door. She looked like she could have been a very nice girl before she found the Hobo Punch. She was quite pretty – in a drunken, disheveled sort of way. She had long brown hair and was wearing a pair of tight, butt-hugging jeans. She wobbled there for a minute doing her best to stand erect and remain in one place.

"Rough sea tonight, huh sailor?" Charlie commented with a bemused grin.

"F'in right it is," she slurred. "And if I don't pee pretty quick there's going to be an ocean of trouble right here in river city." At that moment she glanced to her right and saw the old commode sitting on the porch. "God," she exclaimed. "This is a classy joint! But what the hell! When in Rome as they f'in say. Okay boys, back off and spread out!"

She stepped up - or backed up - to the commode, unbuttoned her pants, pulled down her draws, sat on the commode and peed with a big sigh of relief. When she finished she looked around desperately. Then beamed up at Charlie and me and said. "Fellas, I can take an f'in joke but where the hell is the toilet paper?"

We both looked at her and pointed. "It's in the bathroom just behind that door," we chimed.

She took a gander down to her right towards the bathroom door, then shook her head and mumbled in frustration. "You have got to be shi----g me!"

"Honey please, you are talking to the clean up crew," Charlie said crushing his Lucky Strike on the deck. "A little pee on the back porch is acceptable but any more than that and you're cleaning it up yourself, matey."

The Old Gang and Our First Cottage

Up until the age of sixteen my folks always tried to get the family off for a week or two "at the beach" every year. At sixteen "the gang" took over. The old gang rented a cottage at the beach every year from the time I was 16 until I reached the age of 27. We had a few guys who were old enough to sign the leases in our early days. But as I remember there were many renters who were not all that particular. If you had the money, you got the cottage.

I think we had 40 guys who chipped in for our first all season rental at Hampton Beach. The cottage was called the Marilyn and it was on Island Path. This particular cottage is notorious in the minds of our original renters to this day.

Every evening the floors were littered with bodies. The beds went to the original seven or eight of us who thought up this timeshare idea. On several weekends even the floors would be filled. The bodies then spilled over into the cars in the tiny parking lot.

I remember coming in late and stepping over people to get to my bedroom. When I stepped on somebody and they voiced their disapproval, my response was rather Reaganesque, "Hey listen you, I'm one of the guys who is paying for this place!" The person lying on the floor would usually apologize. It was often necessary to evict strangers from my bed. For the most part they respected their position and found a new spot on the floor.

The Marilyn was down the end of a road and surrounded by a swamp. The cottage was isolated by the swamp which added a certain amount of privacy and mysteriousness to it. The swamp was kept at bay by a large wooden fence. The cottage was really a shack. It leaned to one side. We didn't know if it was sinking into the swamp or just falling over.

The Marilyn was well known to the Hampton Beach Police Department. Most of the cops on the force had been to our home away from home so many times, that we actually befriended a number of them. When a cruiser happened to appear outside our little paradise by the sea, someone would go to the window and then announce whether the officers were friend or foe. If the officer was foe, we usually got a warning about the noise or the loud music and were told to calm it down. Kids like us were important to the beach economic community - for a while at least.

Our little villa by the swamp gained a reputation and became a must-go-to place for the junior crowd. We had guests from all walks of society.

On one occasion an overdressed young man came in with his equally over-dressed girlfriend. The young man knew one of our forty renters and just happened to be in the area. They were gawkers and obviously slumming. The young lady was wide-eyed and clearly astounded. The young man was proud as a peacock to be able to show his date this side of life. Their faces beamed and their eyes rolled around wide and astonished. Clearly they had never seen anything like this before in their lives. I imagine to their minds it was much like a trip to New York's infamous Bowery or some skid row.

Things were going well until a cruiser pulled up outside. One of our full-timers peeked out a window. He turned and gave the "no problem" signal. Our uptown guests, unfortunately, were not familiar with our signals. The young man went to the window and took a peek for himself. He exploded, "It's the police!"

He and his local prom queen began rushing around in every direction. We all sat watching them curiously. Hadn't they ever seen a police cruiser or a cop before? What was with this couple?

By the time our two buddies from the Hampton Beach Police Department came to the door. Rodney and Penelope (not their real names) had vanished.

We all chatted with the cops. They gave us the usual warning about not letting things get out of hand and then they left.

A short time passed and we all began to wonder where our two well dressed tourists had disappeared to. Someone recalled seeing them scurrying out the back door. We wandered out back. We heard some whimpering. It was coming from the swamp-side of the fence. We hiked one of the boys up to take a peek over the fence. There, waist deep in muck and mire, sat our friends Rodney and Penelope.

We lowered them a rope and somehow pulled them both from the soggy, snake ridden mire. He did not look good. She looked much worse. They went home. They had their fill of skid row and the Bowery Boys.

Our season ended abruptly at the Marilyn when we all returned from the Center one evening and found a sign on our front door. Our cottage had been condemned. We weren't even allowed back inside to claim our "valuables." We thought briefly that our rights had been violated and that maybe we could sue somebody. But then on second thought, we decided that we best leave well enough alone.

HAVE YOU READ THESE BOOKS BY

RICHARD EDWARD NOBLE

Hobo-ing America

Honor Thy Father and Thy Mother

The Eastpointer

A Little Something

Noble Notes on Famous Folks

These books are available on www.Amazon.com, the largest internet book seller in the world.

Bookstores, libraries and other vendors can contact Noble Publishing at richardedwardnoble@fairpoint.net or Noble Publishing, box 643, Eastpoint, Fl 32328 for volume discounts.

A standard 40% discount is offered to all buyers ordering four or more books from Noble Publishing – mix and match.

HOBO-ING AMERICA

Seeing the U.S.A. clinging to the elbow of Carol and Dick will be an awakening for most Americans no matter how many times they have toured the U.S.A.

Come along with Carol and Dick and live in the places where Charles Kuralt was afraid to park his bus.

Feel the pain, joy and anger and shake the calloused hands that make America what it is.

See America in its glory and its shame. See it from the highways, the sidewalks and the gutters. Meet Asians, Indians, Jamaicans, Haitians, Mexicans. Meet most of them in one chicken factory in central Arkansas on the third shift.

See America from the bottom of the cracker barrel. Come along with Carol and Dick. Talk to the "Crackers" and fill the barrels.

HONOR THY FATHER AND THY MOTHER

Honor Thy Father and Thy Mother is a tragic novel. The main character is a little boy. The reader learns to understand Richard by listening to his thoughts. We read his mind as he tries to make sense of those around him. We follow Richard's thoughts from ages five to thirteen as he translates the people, the circumstances, and the society around him. The reader will walk through a tragedy of personal, religious and social confusion. Anyone who reads this book will be left with some very difficult impressions and many shocking images that will never go away.

The book is an attempt to distinguish between discipline and abuse, between a spanking and a beating, between being scolded and being harried, between learning and indoctrination. It is a journey through the rational and the irrational.

Honor Thy Father and Thy Mother is also a love story and it is a study in the nature of hate at the same time. It is about family and religion. It is about hard times and depression. It is about alcohol and alcoholism. It is about what is going on in the apartment upstairs or the tenement next door. It is real life – and death.

THE EASTPOINTER

My column *the Eastpointer* appeared each week in the *Franklin Chronicle*. In 2007 I won the first place award for humor from the Florida Press Association.

Eastpoint is in the Florida Panhandle, across the bridge from Apalachicola to the west and a few miles from the town of Carrabelle to the east. All three of these small communities are located in Franklin County on the Gulf Coast.

Franklin County has been, traditionally a seafood community. This volume contains a selection of columns that not only present the ideas and opinions of the author but create a portrait of life in the "sleepy, little fishing village" of Eastpoint.

A LITTLE SOMETHING

A Little Something is a volume of poetry with prose. The volume is divided into several categories – My Hometown, Humor, Love and Other Nice Things, Tenderness and Tears, and On the Serious Side. The poetry is traditional in style and, as with all poetry, covers a wide range of interests and ideas.

BUT, DO YOU LOVE ME

But, do you love me?
And how would I know?
I look into your eyes, but the love doesn't show.
So how ... how would I know?
Days and nights, weeks and years,
Moments of laughter, and a lifetime of tears.

But do you love me?
And how would I know?
Nothing I see would tell me it's so.
We touch, we love, we laugh, we smile.
We cherish the moments, mile after mile.

But do you love me?
And how would I know?
Unless once in a while...
You'd tell me so.

NOBLE NOTES ON FAMOUS FOLKS

Noble Notes on Famous Folks is a book of historical essays. It is not a history book. It is a book about history.

This book contains the opinions, insights and interpretations of the author along with historical facts, quotes and situations.

These are notes that I have accumulated over the years. All these notes were originally written for my own edification and to assist my memory. You might look at this work as my home-schooled college diary or study notes.

I've included in this volume a variety of ancient and modern characters ranging from Constantine to Bill Clinton. Some are treated humorously, some satirically and some seriously.

MEET
RICHARD EDWARD NOBLE

Richard Edward Noble was raised in Lawrence, Massachusetts. He attended St. Rita's grammar school in Lawrence, Central Catholic high school also in Lawrence, Northern Essex Community College in Haverhill and Merrimack College in North Andover.

His mother and father and grandparents – on both sides of the family – were Lawrence textile workers.

Richard lived in Lawrence until the age of twenty-seven and then migrated to Fort Lauderdale, Florida where he met his wife Carol. Richard and Carol have been a team for over thirty-five years. They have both worked a variety of jobs. Richard has been a butcher, a dishwasher, an oysterman, a fruit picker, a restaurant manager and chef and the owner/operator of an ice cream parlor and sandwich shop in Carrabelle, Florida. These experiences and many more were published in Hobo-ing America – A workingman's tour of the U.S.A.

Richard is now retired and working as a writer. He writes fiction, non-fiction and poetry. He publishes a column in a local newspaper. In 2007 he received a first place award for humor from the Florida Press Association for this column.

Richard has a variety of interests – philosophy, history, politics, the American and world labor movements, economics, poetry, music, biography, autobiography and the unique history of Lawrence, Massachusetts.

77885136R00092

Made in the USA
Middletown, DE
27 June 2018